DANGER'S RACE

A HOLLY DANGER NOVEL:
BOOK THREE

AMANDA CARLSON

OTHER BOOKS BY AMANDA CARLSON

Jessica McClain Series:
Urban Fantasy
BLOODED
FULL BLOODED
HOT BLOODED
COLD BLOODED
RED BLOODED
PURE BLOODED
BLUE BLOODED

Sin City Collectors:
Paranormal Romance
ACES WILD
ANTE UP
ALL IN

Phoebe Meadows:
Contemporary Fantasy
STRUCK
FREED
EXILED

Holly Danger:
Futuristic Dystopian
DANGER'S HALO
DANGER'S VICE
DANGER'S RACE
DANGER'S CURE
DANGER'S HUNT

For Paige.
May every adventure be just as exciting as the last.

Chapter 1

"Can we trust this Ned guy?" Bender asked, his voice expressing more than a little grumble. It was just after dawn, and an early riser he wasn't. But the timing couldn't be helped. We were gathered in his shop, the communal place for most of our meetings, to discuss our new mission. We were each taking off in separate directions to find key ingredients Darby needed to concoct a cure for Plush, the pharma-psychotic drug that permanently altered the DNA of users, turning them into mindless pleasure seekers. We would be venturing to places we'd never been, as what Darby needed wasn't available in the city. It was daunting, but we were up for it.

Success was the best—*and likely only*—chance we had to help Mary, an innocent woman who'd been caught up in the dangerous games of zealots and outskirts in this dark city.

Mary was only one among thousands of seekers

who needed our help. But starting with her made sense, as she'd been recently infected and had a high chance of pulling through with no lasting effects.

I stood with my back against the wall, arms crossed. Daze sat in a chair, fiddling with a gadget he'd found on one of the worktables. Lockland had his shoulder braced against the cooling unit, and Bender was situated on his regular stool, a jug of aminos gripped in his fist.

Case stood off to the side, near the hallway we'd just come through. It was strange to have him here, but since he was my partner on this journey, it was necessary.

Darby was back at the Emporium with Ned, the person we were currently discussing, trying to finalize everything so when we arrived back with all the necessary ingredients—hopefully within a few days— he could put the cure together.

"All I can go by is our history together," I told the group. "When I first met Ned, he wanted to make a deal. He wasn't in Hutch's group by choice. Then, two days ago, the day we sent Cozzi off, he took me to Dill's residence and we scoured the place. It was a dump. I'm pretty sure the cockroaches still scurrying around the city have better accommodations. Dill, it seems, was a fairly new recruit to the group and not in the know. Ned was friends with Mary before she was infected and wants to help." I shrugged. "He's agreed to protect Darby and take care of Mary while we're gone. Claire can't get away, and the rest of us are taking off to places unknown. He's trustworthy enough, but I'll go with whatever we decide. He'll walk without issue if we tell him to."

"Ned can stay," Lockland said, shoving off from the cooling unit as he reached into his pocket, withdrawing a small box. "Having somebody look after Mary sounds like a good idea to me." He walked over and placed the item into my now outstretched hand.

"What's this?" I asked as I popped the top off, leaning over to examine it, not believing my eyes. Inside the box, nestled in a piece of soft cloth, sat a very rare status reader. "No way," I exclaimed. "Where did you find this?"

I knew what it was by its shape and color alone. A small white oval made of semigloss polymer. These had been fairly common before the dark days. It had a flat section on the bottom so it could rest on a counter or desktop, which had been the preferred location. They were purported to relay time, temperature, atmospheric readings, and could even detect human matter, all upon request.

People called them "status eggs" for short. I had only a picture to go on, but it did look remarkably like an egg.

Daze hustled to my side, intrigued by what I held in my hand. He made a move to touch it, but I shook my head. "There's a reason it's in this box with the cloth," I told him. "The organic matter on your fingers could contaminate the sensors. It uses NeuDAR technology to take readings." NueDAR was short for neutrino detection and ranging. According to the historical data, the egg sent out neutrinos to do all its detecting. Neutrinos could pass through metal, rock, human bodies, anything. The detector was capable of reading individual atoms when they were struck by a neutrino. "When they were first made, they had some sort of coating on them, but who knows if it's worn off or not? Let's not take any chances." I glanced at Lockland. "Does the voice activation work, or is this one manual only?" It had a switch tucked inside the flat bottom that would display the basic settings on the top of the shell.

Voice activation, as a whole, hadn't held up over the years. The software used to be linked to the central All Voice Database, which was lost, and very few gadgets had their own onboard voice-data systems.

Lockland arched a cagey eyebrow at me. "Give it a try. To power it up, say, 'Reader on.'"

I'd lowered the box in front of Daze. "Go ahead, you try first."

"What should I ask it to do?"

I shrugged. "I don't know. Ask it what the temperature is or how many of us are in the room."

"Okay." Daze licked his lips like he was readying for a long, important oration. I grinned as he cleared his throat and, in a voice several decibels lower than his natural speaking voice, commanded, "Reader on."

Amazingly, the thing popped to life.

An array of colored lights dotted the surface, tiny pinpricks of multicolored brightness blinking faster than I could track.

Everybody gathered around to see this rare piece of technology actually work, including Case.

"Who needs to know the temperature?" Bender grumbled. "It's always cold and rainy. End of story." His attitude belied the fact that his eyes were riveted on the thing, just like everybody else's.

Several low beeps issued out as the lights jumped around on the surface before solidifying into two glowing green numerals. The number fifteen flashed twice, followed by a soft, fluid female voice. "The temperature is fifteen degrees Celsius. The barometer is dropping rapidly. Expect rain."

She'd answered Bender's question—which hadn't really been a question—with a real answer. It was nothing short of amazing, and we all gaped.

"Expect?" Bender snorted. "How about it's raining *now*?"

"Stop spoiling the fun, fun-spoiler," I told him as I nudged Daze. "Go ahead, ask her something else."

"Um," Daze hedged. Then, in the same low, comical baritone, he asked, his lips only centimeters from the thing, "How many people are in the room?"

The egg's lights zoomed around on the surface, shooting off a kaleidoscope of lasers. Several beeps sounded, and the number five flashed. After a second, the woman's voice, which was extremely polished and perfect, which itself was slightly unsettling, flowed out. "I detect five humans within two meters, nine humans within twenty meters, and thirty-four humans, and several invertebrates, within one hundred meters."

Holy shit.

This was by far the most technically advanced gadget I'd ever been in contact with in my life. This egg was top-of-the-line NewGen stuff—the kind of thing that had been extremely common in a world clogged with technology and innovation, but hadn't survived the chaos of the last sixty years because it was too fragile, the systems too intricate, the tech too advanced.

My eyes sought Lockland's. "Did you know it could do that?" My tone was hushed, because hell, this deserved a little reverence. "Is one hundred meters the max it can go?"

"I've played around with it a bit," he said, his tone matching mine, the ode to technology noted. "It seems one hundred meters is as far as it can detect. But this is a military-grade status reader, which means it contains tons of memory and was made to last. From what I've researched, it might have the ability to learn and adapt, as some of these readers had artificial intelligence installed, along with their massive internal database. Civilian status readers accessed the full Interwebs wirelessly, constantly combing for current data. The military needed everything on hand and adaptable in nonaccess events, so they came stocked." He shrugged. "But I'm not sure. Like I said, I haven't had much time to invest in it."

I stared at the thing in my palm.

It was hard to believe something that small and innocuous could manage to contain information like that, but then again, the quantum drive was extremely tiny and held vast amounts of data. Technology before the dark days had been incredible. "Why are you bringing this out now?" I asked. "This is an unbelievable prize. Why give it up?"

Lockland shrugged. "My destination is fairly close. I'm looking for a refinery that used to make clay. Darby is pretty sure it exists within two hundred kilometers of here. Your mission is much harder. We don't even know if kelp grows in the sea anymore. Plus"—his gaze landed on Daze—"the kid grew up with a pico. I thought he might be able figure out what this thing is truly capable of, even better than I could."

I nudged Daze as I lowered the box into his hand. "What do you say? That's pretty high praise. I agree with Lockland. You're definitely smart enough to figure it out."

Daze took the egg from me like it was made of the rarest material on Earth, which it pretty much was. He glanced up, wide-eyed, and addressed Lockland. "I'll make sure nothing happens to it, I promise." He bowed his head to examine his new prize. "I'm pretty sure I can figure it out. I've heard of these before. My dad's pico had lots of information. He was really smart." His chest puffed out, as it always did when he spoke of his father. "I know some stuff."

"That's what I'm counting on," Lockland said. "We're all going to be out of bandwidth frequency, so there'll be no way to get a hold of each other. I don't like it, but there's nothing we can do about it. The status reader will help in your search and keep you safe."

"I'm sure it will," I said, my heart doing one of those still-new-to-me clench-unclench thingies.

The feeling was getting more familiar, but it was still strange. Lockland had given us this gift because he wanted to do everything in his power to ensure we survived. It was a sacrifice, since it would have helped him to stay safe as well.

Bender strode over to a large duffel by the door and hefted it up over his shoulder. "If Darby is wrong about my destination, I'll be back sooner than later. I'm on the hunt for zinc, and he's pretty sure there's some located not too far away. He seems to think he can find everything else he needs in the city. Once I get back, I'll help him gather up the stuff." Bender opened the door. That was our cue to leave. We followed him out into the hallway.

Our crafts were parked on the roof, including Luce, which I was going to keep here for the time being. Nobody messed with Bender or his stuff, so she would be safe.

Once on the roof, we made our way to our respective transports. "After we get back, dealing with Port Station will be our first priority," I told the group. "I don't know how many of Tandor's or Hutch's guys are left over—if any—but if they're still in charge over there, we're going to have to remedy that problem." Dealing with Port Station at a later date wasn't ideal, but Mary needed our help immediately. That came first.

Lockland stood in front of his craft, a decent-looking M5 he called Rose, named for a flower none of us had ever seen bloom. Also, because she'd been red years ago, but had faded to a chalky pink. He kept threatening to recoat her, since we'd amassed cans of colored polycover over the years, but he never followed through. "I have a few contacts looking into the issue in Port Station," Lockland said as he lofted his pilot door. "And Claire's going to send some government people over to investigate under the pretense of making some kind of food trade to see what they can find." Port Station's protein-cake production was a step below ours, if that was even possible. I'd never tasted a single morsel and planned to keep it that way. "I'm optimistic it will be dealt with by the time we get back. According to what Ned said, since Hutch was terminated, any opposition should melt away."

"Fat chance," Bender said, opening the door of his craft, which he'd named Sue, after his mother. Bender never talked about his family, so I had no details other than her first name. "That kinda shit never settles itself. We're going to have to go in with guns blazing to set it to rights, like always."

"Maybe, maybe not," I said. "With no one in charge of Tandor's original group, it might take care of itself. Those guys weren't exactly smart, and if there are no clear leaders to step up, there's a possibility the problem might go away on its own." I watched Case make his way over to Seven's pilot-side door. "Oh, no, you don't," I said, hurrying to catch up. "I'm flying."

He shook his head, peering at me from over the top of his craft. "Nope. I am."

"We agreed that this was my mission," I argued. "Get it? My. Mission. And because I'm in charge, I fly." I mean, it only made sense.

"You two have fun working that out," Bender called as he slammed his door. Lockland already had his props winding up.

Case gave me another look over the roof. It was a mixture of exasperation and irritation. Get used to it, buddy. "We have a minimum of a six-and-a-half-hour flight before we reach my hometown," he said. "I know exactly how to get there."

"And so does your craft," I said, crossing my arms. "All I have to do is punch in the destination, and your data-recorded flight path takes us there."

"I have an idea," Daze quipped from behind me, the status reader clutched protectively against his chest. "How about Case flies for the first three hours, and you fly for the next three hours? That way you can both avoid flight fatigue."

"What do you know about flight fatigue?" I asked, raising a single eyebrow. Flight fatigue was real, especially over long distances. But nobody traversed very many kilometers at a time anymore, so it was rarely discussed. Fatigue happened because the environment out your front window never changed:

same brightness, same color sky, same rain. It tended to dull the senses and, from what I'd heard, make you groggy.

Daze eased into the passenger side through the open door. "My dad had a craft," he told me as he crawled inside, heading to the backseat. "It was a C9. That kind was known for safety. My dad liked to be safe. He wrote about traveling from the South back to the city a bunch of times on the pico, and about how he had flight fatigue. He almost crashed once."

It seemed there was a lot yet to uncover about Daze and his prior life, and what he'd found on the pico.

I met Case's gaze over the top of Seven. "Fine. We go with the kid's plan," I said begrudgingly. "You take the first three. I'll take the next. When's the last time you were down South?"

Case answered as he got in. "A couple months ago, right around the time Tandor rolled into town. Before that, I hadn't been back in a while. I'm not sure who's left, as Tandor took a bunch with him, but I know for sure a few of my sustainee siblings stayed behind. They should know something."

Our main objective was to find out where Tandor called home and head there, hoping to find the sodium alginate, either in powder or seaweed form. From what Darby could figure out from the notes on the quantum drive, Tandor's father was the scientist behind the data, so we assumed Tandor had taken the drive and the supplies when he'd left.

It was a long shot, but it was all we had.

Punching a button, Case started up the craft, and the props whirred to life. He lofted us smoothly into the air. "If my siblings know anything, they'll talk," he stated confidently. "If not, I'll make them."

If Case couldn't, I would.

Chapter 2

"You did that on purpose." I crunched over the broken ground, pocked with holes filled with red-hued water. Case had finally landed Seven, and we were trading spots after four hours of mind-numbing travel. "There were plenty of places you could've set her down before this one."

We passed each other at the front of the craft. He grunted, "There's a hard-and-fast rule when traveling outside city limits—always land where you know it's safe. Otherwise, you can get into trouble."

I stopped, spreading my arms wide as I glanced at the topography around me, which mirrored all the kilometers we'd previously traversed. "You can't tell me that you recognize this particular patch of land. It all looks the same from the sky. Gnarled, scarred trees and dead, barren earth as far as the eye can see."

He stopped in front of the passenger door, glancing at me over the top. "This happens to be an old farm where my Sun Optimist sustainer family dug an underground shelter for a season. I was thirteen years old at the time. Still looks the same."

My eyes ranged over the empty expanse of land, spotting nothing in particular. I peered back at Case. "Prove it."

His visor was down, but I could see his expression change to surprise. "You want to see our underground shelter?"

"Why not? It would certainly go a long way in validating your past." Case had relayed some of his backstory to me in an effort to cement some trust between us, but it'd been his word against nothing. There'd been no way to prove what he'd said was real—until now. Not to mention, he'd already played me a couple of times, so it was worth it to me to see if this part of his story checked out. If it didn't, we'd have an issue.

He leaned forward, his elbows on the craft, his face tight. "I didn't lie to you."

I shrugged. "Your story was impossible to prove, until now."

Daze poked his head out of the craft. "Can we? Can we go see it? That would be so cool."

The kid was already climbing out. "We can," I told him. "But leave the status reader in the craft, and while you're at it, shut down Seven for me."

Daze did as I asked and hopped out, chipper as ever, not showing any signs of fatigue. I had to blink my eyes a few times to adjust to seeing darker colors.

The clouds were a lot brighter than land.

I glanced at Case, inclining my head. "Lead the way."

His facial expression didn't change as he turned and made his way toward a copse of trees. One that looked just like all the others lining this patch of land he said used to be a farm.

Daze and I trudged after him.

We passed through several groupings of trees just like the first ones. I couldn't pick out any defining features of the area. Then, abruptly, Case came to a stop. The tips of his boots touched a large square of graphene set directly into the dirt.

The door was old and battered and looked as though it'd been there a long time, weathering years of rain—small divots of liquid had permanently gathered in the honeycombed pattern. I'd never seen a horizontal door set in the earth before. "How did you get it to stay in there like that?" I asked.

Case leaned over and grabbed the handle, grunting as he hoisted the door upward. "It's held up by a network of framing below. The hardest part was making it waterproof. The support structure had to be overlapped perfectly for it to work."

This seemed like a random place to build a shelter. "How did they pick this exact location?"

"My sustainer father, Scott, was always trying to be strategic. He felt that when the sun finally decided to grace us with its presence again, we would need a farm with enough land to support the fifteen people that made up the group. He was very careful about choosing the spot. There's a river near here and remnants of an old farmhouse fifty meters to the north. He always selected a place with ample tree cover, but none with roots too close. It had to be undetectable from the sky. That's why the entrance is set into the ground."

"Sounds like a lot of thought went into it," I said, impressed. "Did everyone in the group believe the sun would eventually shine?" It was a valid question. In order to be a part of a group like that, the members would have to believe, at least a little bit.

Daze moved toward the open door, glancing down into the darkness. "I would've believed." He slid off his helmet. "And if I didn't, I would've wanted to believe. Having a family is everything."

Case studied Daze for a few moments. "I didn't believe. But you're right, I wanted to believe. And there's power in that. Building these shelters kept us busy, and when we were done, we had a place to stay out of the rain. We followed Scott and Annabelle, my sustainer mother, all around this region. It wasn't a great life, but it was good enough. It taught me to be a hard worker."

We all descended the stairs.

The kid went first, followed by Case, then me.

Daze's voice carried from below. "This is so cool!" he cried, followed by, "Are those real animal bones?"

The interior was fairly spacious, which was surprising. The hole had obviously been dug by hand, the dirt laboriously removed. Random panels of metal, all different sizes and types, some smooth, some corrugated, had been secured to make walls. The floor was nothing more than packed earth with a few metal pieces strewn about. There were a few rickety chairs, some very crude eating utensils, and not much else.

My nostrils crinkled as I took in a breath. The air hadn't been disturbed in a long while. It was musty, with a strong undertone of decaying matter.

"Yes, those are real animal bones," Case said to Daze. "My parents had us digging a lot, so we encountered bones frequently. When we found a full skeleton, we always brought it back and tried to re-create the animal it once was. I believe that one was a fox, based on old pictures we'd seen."

"Can I touch it?" Daze asked, stooping in front of an object that had been glued together with clear hydrogel. It didn't resemble a skeleton, per se, more like a sculpture of eerie dead bones.

"Be my guest," Case said.

I wandered toward one of the walls, extending my hand to touch the rough surface. My gloves came away wet. The ground above was always saturated, so seepage was a given. It was dark down here, the only opening casting any brightness was the one we'd just come through. I flipped on one of my shoulder lights so we could see better. "The space is deceiving from up top. This is more than big enough to hold fifteen people." I turned in a circle. "But where did everybody sleep?"

Case walked to the other side and pulled open a metal panel. I followed him in as he went through. It was a quarter the size of the other room. Inside, mats were laid out a meter apart, moldy and half eaten with age. Rough shelving units had been dug into the walls, and a few items lay there, long forgotten.

"This is where we slept while we were here," he said. "Building shelters gave us a concrete goal to aim for. Without the tasks in front of us, our lives would've been stagnant. Life without purpose can lead to madness, which my sustainer parents understood." He turned on his own shoulder light, and a double blue glow effused the small space.

I walked over to one of the shelves. "I'm glad you had something to keep you busy."

"Back then, I knew what we were doing was pointless, but it was good to have work to do." He picked up a small item that had been left behind, turning it over in his hands. "It kept us focused on something more than just survival. I don't miss it." He glanced around. "How could I miss a place like this? But I do miss having the connection I felt to these people when I woke up every day."

I crouched by one of the mats on the floor. It'd been woven out of carbon fiber and was frayed at the ends and coated with mud. Not much protection between it and the hard ground. "It was just me and my mom for the first eight years. After that, it was Claire and Bender. Then my family gradually grew to include Lockland and Darby." As I stood, I chuckled. "I stumbled on Darby one day in passing. It was a chance meeting. He'd been trying to find his way to Government Square, but he'd gotten lost and wound up too close to The Middle. He'd only been on his own for about a year at that point. His parents had passed away fairly close to each other. He was barely twenty years old. He was—and still is—the most innocent among us. Lockland was brought in by Bender." I turned toward Case, the blue light too dim for me to see him clearly. Maybe that made it easier for me to speak about my family. Sharing wasn't my specialty. "Without them, I wouldn't bother getting out of bed in the morning. Daze is right. All that really matters is family. It binds us together and gives us a greater purpose, no matter what we're doing—whether it's building a shelter or scavenging for goods, fighting shitty zealots, or finding a cure for a drug that has ravaged the minds of innocent humans. Without those bonds, none of it matters."

Case looked as though he might say something, but instead tucked the trinket he'd been holding into his pocket and turned and walked out of the room.

When I emerged, Daze had the skull of the dead animal in his hands and was bouncing around excitedly. "I don't think this is a fox," he said. "I think it might be too big. But I don't know for sure. There are some animal charts on the pico. I can't wait to look. Case said I could bring it with. Do you think it's a fox?" He held it up to me like an offering so I could inspect it.

"I don't know, kid." I grinned. "It just looks like a skull to me. But I do know it's time to go. We need to make it to our destination before full dark."

"Okay," Daze said as he trailed after me toward the stairs. "Maybe we can come back another time."

It wasn't likely, but I wouldn't say never. "We'll see."

Once we were all outside, Case lowered the door back into the earth. Without comment, we followed him back to the craft.

I climbed into the pilot side, and when everybody was secure, I took us into the air. Making sure the digital readout flashed *South,* I increased Seven's speed and altitude. Behind us, Daze settled in with the status reader, murmuring to the egg like they were the opposite ends of two magnets drawn together by a mutual quest for information.

For the next hour, we skimmed the same dead forest intermixed with barren stretches of earth. "Where are the cities?" I asked Case. "There should be something remaining. A broken building or two. Leftover concrete from old roads. Something."

"The path we're on skirts all cities. The ones near the coast are all gone, reduced to nothing more than dust, and those inland are shells, their resources having been picked over long ago. But that doesn't mean they're vacant. Tribes are still trying to survive there. Some would do anything to get their hands on a craft. I was almost shot down twice flying over a city. They don't have much, but they do have weapons. Weapons, for the most part, were designed to last."

I knew people existed out here, but that sounded harrowing. "How come no one has tried to help them?" My voice rang with some of the indignation that was bubbling up. "Why doesn't our government send people out to find these folks and bring them back to the city?"

Case gave me a look before he answered, one that seemed weary. "We're hundreds of kilometers away from the main city, crafts are limited, and they can only carry so many people. Second, the city doesn't have resources for its own people, much less bringing in more mouths to feed and people to clothe and take care of. It isn't sustainable. Plus, the tribes, for the most part, would be hostile. They've been living on their own since the beginning of the dark days. Being forced to integrate into a different way of life would be difficult. Their instincts would be to hoard supplies and cut themselves off from everything else."

I sighed. He was right, of course. But that didn't make it much better. "I get it on a rational level. But on a humanitarian level, it's not right. We're all human, trying to scrape by with our meager resources. We all deserve a chance. Including those not lucky enough to live near a well-populated area when disaster struck."

"I agree. Maybe if the elite hadn't taken most of the essentials, we could've worked toward that point. But right now, that's not happening. It would take a huge amount of supplies and a task force to get these people to the city, neither of which we have."

I narrowed my gaze. "We? You're a refugee to the city, remember? An outskirt who decided to stay. What makes you any different than those tribes out there looking for a chance at a better life?"

He grinned. "Because I come with my own supplies. I'm not a drag on resources, nor am I a threat to anyone's well-being."

I snorted. "You've been a threat to me since the moment you threw me out a second-story window."

"Not a threat—a *savior*. If I hadn't been there, you would've died."

I was about to rail on his ignorance but saw he was laughing. "It's a good thing you're easily entertained," I grumbled. "And if you hadn't interfered, I would have been fine."

"Whatever you say."

I chose to ignore him, as I wasn't in the mood to be baited. Instead, I focused on the view out my windshield. We would reach Case's old town in a couple hours. We were planning on waiting until first thing in the morning to talk to his siblings who'd stayed behind. "How are you planning to get your siblings to talk if they don't want to?" I asked, curious about what tactics he was going to employ.

Before Case could reply, the status reader announced, "At your present velocity, you will encounter an electrical storm in forty-seven seconds."

Chapter 3

I spotted the first electrical pulse in the distance exactly three seconds after the egg had uttered her smooth, silky words. It was shockingly bright and lasted only a split second.

Before this, I'd witnessed only two electrical storms in my entire life. Once, when I was around five, my mother had taken me to see the streaks brighten the sky during the solstice. I remembered it'd been the solstice, because it was the second day in a row with no rain and longer nights. She'd made me wear a filter mask over my nose and mouth to keep the iron dust out. I hated those masks. They were uncomfortable for an adult, but when I was five, they'd been smothering and almost as big as my face.

The second time, I'd been in my teens. I'd been salvaging a little farther outside the city than usual, in an old manufacturing plant. The facility had been thoroughly picked over and had ended up being a waste of my time. I had been ready to leave when it started, so I stayed put until it passed. I might or might not have taken cover under a few layers of ceiling tiles that had been conveniently stacked on the ground—or that I might've torn down out of fear. It was hard to remember all the details.

I learned later on that the reason lightning storms were so rare was because the iron particles and other mineral deposits in the atmosphere didn't allow voltage to build up. Instead, it provided a constant dissipation path.

In front of us, several bolts of light blinked within the clouds. It looked like someone was rapidly punching a power button on and off. I gasped, my hands tightening around the controls. It was nothing short of terrifying.

"The craft is fully grounded," Case murmured, his voice low and steady. "Even a direct strike can't hurt us. The frame has aluminum integrated throughout. We're safe."

"Yeah, tell that to the weather," I said quietly. Somehow, aluminum, one of the softest, most pliable metals, didn't seem like much of a match against jagged rods of concentrated electricity powerful enough to damage a megascraper.

"Did you see that one?" Daze exclaimed from his new position wedged between our shoulders.

"Yes, I did," I said. Blistering white light that could burn us to a crisp was hard to miss.

"It's amazing," he cooed, his tone appropriately

awe-filled. "I've never seen an electrical pulse storm before. I didn't even think they were real." Leave it to Daze to think something that could kill us was amazing.

My hands had a mind of their own. They gripped the levers so tightly that if my gloves had been off, my knuckles would have been bright white. "I've only seen two," I told Daze. "But never up this close."

"These storms happen in the South because the rocks and dust caught in the upper atmosphere are not uniformly spread out," Case said in an irritatingly calm manner, like this was all completely normal. "There are pockets where the mass is thinner or even nonexistent. If there's a big enough void for a substantial amount of time, electricity can build up."

"How could you know something like that?" I asked. There was no real way of telling where the rocks were or weren't, as they were occluded one hundred percent of the time. "Nobody has seen past the cloud cover since the meteor struck."

Case shrugged as a white shock of light rocketed out less than a hundred meters in front of us, arcing down toward the ground. "I know"—he leaned back in his seat—"because electrical storms are common in some pockets of the South. And if you apply logic, the only thing that makes any sense is that there's no iron buildup where they occur."

"But my point"—which was completely awesome—"is that we can't know for sure. You're just guessing, and even if there are empty spaces up there, they have to be continually moving and shifting, so it would be nearly impossible to pinpoint a particular pattern."

"True," he agreed, but not before I saw him flinch as a strike blinked out of the clouds in front of us. He wasn't immune after all. Though I did appreciate the tough façade. If both of us were freaking out, things could take a quick turn. "But from what I've seen, they move in reliable patterns, either because of the wind or possibly atmospheric pressure. From my hometown, you can witness a storm in the same location in the sky each season."

Suddenly, Daze's arm shot into the space between us as he asked, "What's that?"

"Where?" I said. "What do you see?" I'd been too focused on the clouds to look at much else.

"That big building on the ground. It looks like some kind of—"

Case lunged toward the controls, his hands gripping mine painfully as he yanked the lever upward, shooting us up impossibly close to the electricity-filled clouds. "What the *hell* are you doing?" I shouted, trying to shoulder him out of the way. It didn't work. He swore as he kept increasing our altitude, not answering me. "Case!" My voice became panicked. "You can't take us into the clouds. We could be hit by debris falling from above. Plus, there's a fucking storm swirling around us."

Cloud flight was off-limits for a number of reasons, but mostly because you couldn't dodge what you couldn't see. Small pieces of iron caught in the atmosphere fell from the sky often enough for it to be an issue. They could be anywhere. And when the craft was moving at such a high speed, even encountering something tiny could be cataclysmic.

"We have to take our chances in the clouds," he ground out. "A pulse storm is better than flying over that." He nodded downward as his grip increased. Seven began to be enveloped by the first tendrils of vapor. It would be only seconds before she was fully consumed.

I glanced down at the large building we were passing at a quick clip. It was intact. Judging by Case's actions, it was a serious threat. Right as the clouds began to obscure it from view, Case's death grip on my hands began to ease.

"You can let go now." My voice was short.

Case leaned back in his seat, finally relinquishing control. "You were supposed to punch in the flight path before you took off."

The craft was now fully emerged in the wispy whiteness. Around us, lightning blinked every few seconds. "If you remember, you're the one who flew the first three hours," I said, my attention laser-focused on us not dying. Visibility was minimal, so I wouldn't have very much warning if something appeared in front of us. I wasn't fond of those odds. "If it wasn't logged correctly, it's your fault." Every craft for the past hundred years had been manufactured with a flight-path recorder. It allowed the pilot to access any coordinates you'd flown before, program new ones, measure distances, and more. Back when satellites had been operational, once the flight path was set, the craft could follow it automatically. Without that automated capability today, we had to keep our eyes on the monitor, which would blink if we were off course. I'd seen no blinking to indicate such a thing. "And can you please explain to me what we're running from?"

With his head braced against the seat, Case said, "Remember when I told you about the militia I was involved with?" Tension radiated off of him. "The one that recruited me when I was sixteen?"

"Yeah." No story was ever good when it contained the word *militia*. Case had been recruited under false pretenses, and he'd been horribly abused. He'd been saved by a man named Dixon, who'd wiped out the militia, saving only Case.

"Not all the members were killed."

"And that building is tied to them?"

"Yes. The remaining members joined up with another militia, and over the last six years, they've grown." He closed his eyes. "That's their headquarters. How we got here is beyond me."

The pulse storm was thankfully dying down, or we were flying out of it. Either way, relief was a welcome emotion. "The flight plan was your responsibility," I reiterated.

He tilted his head toward mine, his eyes tired. Flight fatigue could definitely be setting in. "You're right. I know the route by sight. When we changed places, I meant to tell you to log it in. I wasn't paying attention. You're not that far off the route, less than twenty kilometers, but it was enough to bring us within their sights."

"Do you think they spotted us before we reached the clouds?" I asked.

"Time will tell. But my guess is yes. They have spotters."

"How worried should I be?" I asked. "On top of, you know, already worrying about a chunk of iron punching through the craft and tearing it to shreds." My eyes were locked outside the windshield, where the horizon would've been visible if we hadn't been ensconced in clouds. It seemed we'd made it clear of the storm. I hadn't seen any more pulses in the last minute or so.

"Fairly worried." He ran a hand over his face.

"Okay, well," I started, "we can't go back in time. What's done is done. Hopefully, they didn't spot us. But even if they did, I'm getting us out of the clouds now. I don't want to take any more chances." A muffled female voice came from the backseat. The status reader was trying to get a message out, but nobody had asked her a question. I cocked my head, picking up a few words. "What did she say?" Out of the corner of my eye, I watched as Daze brought her forward, taking off the top of the box. "Did you ask her something a while ago?"

Daze shook his head. "No."

"Did you hear what she said?"

"Only at the end. I think she said something about a craft."

That's the word I'd heard, too. I'd begun to lower us out of the clouds when Case reached over and stilled my hand. His grip wasn't as painful this time, but still irritating. He glanced at Daze. "Ask her to repeat it."

Daze raised the box closer to his face. "Please repeat your last sentence."

A moment later, she said, "An unknown craft is in the vicinity."

I glanced at the dash. Nothing was blinking to alert us that there was anything in the area, which meant it was more than three kilometers away. Either that, or whatever it was had all its radio frequencies shut down.

"How far away is the craft?" I asked the status reader.

She replied immediately. "Closing in at seven kilometers." The words *closing in* weren't what I wanted to hear in this particular situation. Before any of us had a chance to react, the reader said, "Six point five kilometers and closing."

That meant the craft was moving extremely fast. Faster than we were.

I accelerated, pushing Seven's speed above two hundred kilometers per hour, which was her max without help.

"We're going to have to engage a hydro-boost," Case stated calmly, like it would be normal to boost in a place where we couldn't see. I was about to respond that he was out of his mind when he held up his hand. "A boost is the only way to get out of range.

They know we're here. They will shoot this craft down as soon as they can, kill us if the crash doesn't, take our supplies, and spit on our corpses." That wasn't a pleasant thought. "Once we're outside of radio range, we land and shut down our frequency outputs and hope for the best." His eyes were tight, his gaze unfaltering. "Hitting a stray rock would give us a better chance of survival than encountering them."

From the egg, "Six kilometers and closing."

"Shit." I had to make a decision. Case was right. My hand slapped down on the appropriate button that would launch us out of there.

The explosion started instantaneously as the hydrogen chamber positioned at the back of the craft rocketed us forward, the clouds blurring past. After ten more seconds of white-knuckle flying, Case reached over and switched the entire dash panel off.

Everything went dark.

We could still fly, but we had no readings, nothing to tell us which direction we were heading, or if there were any crafts in the area. Those were all determined by radio frequency.

He had the nerve to grin. "Even though we're going dark, we have something that they don't." He turned to Daze. "Check and see what the status reader has to say."

Daze's voice came out as shaky as my insides felt. "Are there any crafts close by?"

I held my breath. The hydro-boost was starting to

slow, but without a digital readout, I couldn't tell by how much.

The egg answered, "There are no crafts in the area."

Exhaling loudly, I made a move to lower altitude and get us the hell out of the clouds, when Case reached over to interfere again, but this time I was ready.

My arm shot out, my hand encircling his wrist like a vise. My attitude was running toward feral, adrenaline making me hyperaware. I yanked him close. "Hey, Case, do you know how to sew a hand back on after it's been severed by a laser? If the answer is no, then you need to back off." His eyes met mine, the ends tightening slightly. "I couldn't care less if you think my piloting skills are subpar." My jaw closed, the rest of it coming out in a growl. "Give me a verbal command, and I'll follow it. Touch the controls again, and I will take out my Gem and shoot you. Do you understand what I'm saying?"

He eased back, and I let go of his arm.

After a moment, he said, "Before we reveal ourselves, head straight for a few more minutes. Once we descend, there should be a short mountain range within sight. Not sure which side it will be on. As soon as we're over it, we need to land and stay put for the next twelve hours. I know a location that can keep us sheltered."

I felt like objecting, insisting on continuing to our destination, because we had a schedule to keep if we wanted to aid Mary. But decided against it. It was probably a good idea to show him that I would keep my word, and protecting ourselves from this militia was a priority. If we were shot down or killed by them, there was no helping anyone.

"Fine," I said. "But keep your hands to yourself if you value working limbs."

Chapter 4

Once we were finally out of the clouds, my heart began to beat regularly once again. The rush of adrenaline, along with everything else, had left me a little lightheaded and shaky. But I wasn't about to announce my condition, because I was smart like that.

From behind me, the egg stated, "Female at one meter in distress. Heart rate one hundred fourteen beats per minute. Blood pressure one hundred seventy-four systolic, ninety-two diastolic. Rapid respiration. Nutrition and hydration deficient. Seek aid immediately."

I frowned. The egg just outed my heightened anxiety like it was her job to snitch on me. "Why did she say that?" I grumbled. "Nobody asked her for any information."

Daze shrugged, still wedged between our seats. "I don't know."

"Lockland said that the status reader could learn

things on its own," I said. "What have you two been chatting about all this time?"

Daze hemmed and hawed for a good ten seconds before answering. "I swear, I was just trying out a few things. I didn't mean to access her full capabilities!"

I sighed. I would've run a hand over my face if both hands weren't already busy flying a craft at top speed. "And accessing her full capabilities means…what exactly?" How did this kid figure out the intricacies of a complicated status reader in under four hours? That was the real question.

"She has LiveBot software."

"Daze"—my tone was weary—"we're going to need more than that. I'm not Darby. I know LiveBot technology had the ability to mimic human behavior, and human robots that used it were called LiveBots or Humanoids. But that's about it." Case gestured to the right, and I turned to follow his prompt.

"Um," Daze hedged once again. "It means I gave her some commands, and she adjusted."

"How exactly did she adjust?" I dropped down toward a patch of ground where Case was indicating he wanted me to set down, lowering altitude accordingly. It was a fairly small swath of land ringed with large, blackened trees. I hadn't reengaged the radio frequencies yet, as I didn't want to take any chances of being discovered, but I was seasoned enough to do it without readouts.

"I gave her the freedom option," Daze finally replied.

The status reader quipped, like she was part of our conversation, "All things, living and nonliving, should live freely."

I raised a single eyebrow as far as it would go and turned toward Daze, who wouldn't meet my eyes. "You set her free? As in, she can do and say what she wants?" I was a little astounded that something so small and round and polymer even had the capacity to do such a thing. And what did *free* exactly mean? "Can't you just unfree her?" Knowing she could insert herself into our conversation at any time was a little unsettling.

"I tried," he replied meekly, finally tilting his head up. "Sorry, Holly."

I engaged Seven's landing gear, bringing her down softly. One small bounce and we were grounded. I shut her off. "Was that all the murmuring I heard back there?"

"Yeah," he said. "I got a little carried away. I've read about LiveBots before, and when I asked her if she was one, she answered yes. LiveBots, before the dark days, were made to look just like us. They had lifelike skin and hair and everything." His voice grew animated, his words rushing out. "And once their software was paired with a particular person and language, they adapted really fast. At least that's what it said in my dad's computer. There were pictures of them, too. I wish I could've seen one in real life. That would've been so cool."

I shifted in my seat, turning to glance out the

window at the towering trees. They were all dead, of course, but they were the biggest I'd ever seen. Hard to believe such majestic beauty had been reduced to nothing but black skeletons. "You're going to have to work on shutting her up when necessary," I told Daze as I lifted the door. "She's a distraction and could get us into trouble at the wrong time."

As if on cue, the status reader said, "Holly, female, stats normalizing. Heart rate and blood pressure within acceptable range. Nutrition and hydration remain deficient."

I gave the kid a look, inclining my head just a bit so he understood my meaning, and got out of the craft. If he couldn't control the status reader, the status reader could disappear for a while. I was fairly certain I heard Case covering up a chuckle as he exited, but I decided to ignore it. If the egg could share my vitals with the world, it could certainly share his.

Daze nodded vigorously as he followed me out, the box clutched against his chest. "I will. I promise. I named her Maisie." He continued after he extracted himself from the craft, "After my mom. Her name was Maylynn. Everybody called her Maisie. My dad's name was Robert. Like my first name. I was named after him." He stuck his chin out, daring me to counter his choice of moniker for the reader.

"Maisie's a good choice, kid. I'm sure your mom would be honored." I turned in a circle, glancing up. Over the tops of the trees, crags of a small mountain range were visible. I'd never seen a mountain up close before. The peaks weren't as massive as the ones on my wall screen at my residence in the canals—one of the only working screens in the city, that I knew of— but it was still unbelievably impressive. I was momentarily lost in my own world.

Maisie fixed that. "I detect three humans within three meters, zero humans within one hundred meters, several invertebrates, and no crafts."

"Thanks for that," I muttered, thankful she'd switched topics.

"I kind of like it," Case cracked as he moved off to the right. "She's calm and sensible, and she's adequately anticipating our needs, feeding us useful information."

Cool rain pinged my helmet, coming down harder than a drizzle. I flipped the visor down with a snap. "Calm and sensible?" I called after him. "Rather than excitable and irrational, like a real person?" In a lower tone, I muttered, "Of course she's calm and sensible, she's a *robot*." The trees seemed even larger as we moved closer. "Where are we? Please tell me there's another underground shelter nearby."

Case tossed over his shoulder, "Even better, there's a cave stocked with supplies right through here."

Before following him through the trees, I walked around the back of the craft and opened the trunk compartment, grabbing out a large micro-carbon fiber backpack, durable yet pliable, and a jug of water. I nodded to Daze, who was smart enough to have already strapped his pack onto his back. "Here, take this." I handed the kid an extra thermal blanket. If Case wanted anything else, he'd have to come back and get it.

My pack included another blanket, a graphene aerogel headrest, a small ultrasonic whisk to heat up water, a change of clothes, and some other miscellaneous items. Daze's pack was mostly filled with food in the form of the packs of dried flakes we'd found at the barracks. Just add water, and you had instant protein mush.

At least we wouldn't starve to death.

By the time we caught up with Case, he was half a kilometer down a narrow path through the trees. Other than the pines and a few large rocks dotting the expanse, the ground was barren and muddy, puddles everywhere, some of them deep. The rain rushed down harder here than we were used to in the city. More of a cascade than a drizzle. "How much farther?" I called.

"We're here," he said, disappearing over a small incline.

At the precipice, I stopped to evaluate. It wasn't a sheer drop like the gorge back home. It was a gradual slope, but it still meant we had to make our way down a wet hill. "Daze, grab on to some of the skinny tree trunks as we go," I told the kid. "It's slippery."

We watched as Case maneuvered around a large boulder just below us and dropped out of sight. I scrambled onto the rock after him and poked my head over, spotting the cave entrance below.

It was bigger than I'd expected.

I tossed my legs over the edge and dropped down roughly two meters, landing solidly on a narrow walkway. The slope continued down in front of me, but it wasn't sheer—meaning if we tumbled off, it would suck, but it wouldn't kill us. I waited for Daze to poke his head over, then I gestured to my left. "Go that way, shimmy down the side. It will be easier than jumping."

He nodded, making it around the side to where I was standing in less than a minute.

The constant, streaming rain formed a flowing curtain of liquid across the entrance. I ducked through, Daze right behind me.

We were met with stacks of boxes of supplies lined up tightly against the walls. I stopped to assess the space. Most of the containers had markings, and as I moved closer, I could see they were dated before the dark days and looked military, even though there were no markings explicitly denoting them as such.

"This is so *cooool*," Daze cooed as he wandered ahead of me. "I've never been in a cave before." We each took off our packs and set them on the ground, propped against the rocky wall.

I addressed Case, who was rummaging through a large bin. "Is this a militia storage facility?"

Case tugged out a large, shimmering piece of fabric. Reflective cloth. I could tell by the fluidity that it was extremely well made. The cheap stuff was chunky and crackled. "It could've been once upon a time," he said. "This was one of Dixon's locations. He has them all up and down the coast." Case had told me about Dixon, the militia man who had rescued him and become his mentor years ago. It was because of Dixon that Case knew about the barracks he'd first taken me to. It seemed Case's resources were vast, which felt a little unsettling. There was so much about this man I didn't know. He strode past me, the material bunched under an arm, not stopping. "You can thank me anytime." He made his way out of the cave, his trench coat flapping behind him as he headed back to the craft to cover it up so anything that happened to fly over would have a hard time detecting it.

It wasn't foolproof, but it would help.

"Why should I thank you for trying to fix the fact you forgot to enter the flight plan? I'll thank you when I damn well feel like it," I grumbled as I wandered around, inspecting things.

I found a few months of survival rations, a couple cots folded up against the wall, two empty metal file cabinets, a battered macro-screen, and several pieces of broken furniture. "Why would anyone lug all this crap down here?" I muttered. This would've been a temporary shelter at best, and carrying things down that slope would be hazardous to anyone's health. Food and water and, possibly, one cot. But file cabinets and broken furniture? It didn't make sense.

Daze spotted something tucked under a shallow overhang. "Look," he said excitedly. "It's a box of guns." Sure enough, the kid had found an aluminum box with multiple barrels poking out of the top.

He reached in to grab one, and I stilled his hand. "Not so fast," I said, gently steering him out of the way. "Old laser guns are extremely unpredictable. We don't know how long these have been sitting here. If they still have a charge in them, they could go off without warning."

As I carefully pulled a gun out to inspect it, Case returned.

"Hey," Daze called to him. "We found guns. Holly thinks they might be unstable. Do you know how long they've been here?" His voice held eagerness, like even if they worked, I was just going to allow him to take his pick. That wasn't happening.

Bender had given him a laser when they'd come in to save us from Hutch and his crew, but that'd been an exception—we'd needed all the help we could get in that situation. But training with a laser gun took time. You had to be careful not to aim at any reflective surfaces, or the bounce back could kill you. Then you had to time your finger on the trigger just right. A small tap would produce a short blast of light. A longer pull would produce a steady stream, which ended when the fuel cell was discharged. Each gun had its own quirks. In order to be successful, you had to know how long a standard blast would last. If you didn't, a small movement in your wrist could prove deadly.

In other words, using a laser gun was an art form.

"Even if they're not that old," I told him, "you're not inheriting a laser gun from this box until we get time to practice." I set the gun in my hand down and eased another one out of the box. I flipped the housing up and was relieved to see it didn't have a fuel cube inside, just like the last one.

Case stopped behind us. "I have no idea how long they've been here. I've only visited this place once before. Dixon never said much about the stuff in here. We were in and out quickly, only using it as a temporary shelter." He leaned over my shoulder and took out a gun.

I checked four more, all of them without cubes.

A laser gun wouldn't operate without a nano-carbon cube of concentrated hydrogen. I stood, brushing my gloved hands against my legs. "I don't think any of them are operational. You can keep looking," I told Daze, "but be extremely careful. Did you see how I opened them up to check?"

He nodded. "I'll be careful. I promise."

"I'm going to keep checking the place out." The cave was at least thirty meters in diameter. I wandered to the other side and noticed a darker area to my left. It was the opening to a skinny tunnel.

I flipped my visor down and stepped through the passageway. There was enough light to allow me to see with infrared. Metal storage lockboxes, less than a meter long and half as tall, lined the narrow, rocky walls, stacked six or seven high. They were engraved with a decorative logo.

A familiar logo.

I flicked on my shoulder light and leaned over to read one.

Surprised, I took a step back. Bliss Corp's distinctive signature, a large B and C intertwined, with a curved arrow shooting out from the bottom of the C and making a sharp turn to join the two letters through the middle, was clearly imprinted on all the containers.

The makers of Plush.

The drug we were on a quest to try to find a cure for.

A shadow darkened the mouth of the tunnel as Case walked in. I stood on my tiptoes to grab the cool metal container on top of the stack. It was heavier than I thought it would be for its size. I had to flex my muscles to make sure I didn't drop it.

Once it was on the ground, I tried to pry open the lid. It wouldn't budge. "Damn," I grumbled. "It's locked from the inside." Which wasn't a surprise, since they were standard, professional-grade lockboxes. "All these containers are engraved with the Bliss Corp logo. You wouldn't happen to know what's in them, would you?"

Case shook his head as he crouched beside me. "I've never seen them before. Like I said, I've only been here once. And, let's just say, I wasn't in an investigative state of mind. Can you get it open?" That likely meant that Case had been injured or running from something. If he wasn't going to divulge on his own, I wasn't going to ask.

"Companies used these boxes to keep their valuables safe. They were fairly standard before the dark days. It's either secured with a mag-strip or a frequency key. My guess is frequency." Securing things in lockboxes became the norm to try to thwart computer hackers. A hacker could pop a digital lock from afar, and did routinely. It had been a major problem before the dark days. Anything computer-operated had been fair game. The government had tried to crack down on hackers—the jail time for hacking was twenty years minimum—but there had been no stopping them. Companies like Bliss Corp had been forced to spend billions to keep themselves and their secrets safe.

My hand automatically went to reach inside one of my handy pockets before I realized I wasn't wearing my vest. I swore. Dill, the asshole, had stolen my favorite article of clothing. I'd gotten him back by activating a radium ball inside it, but that meant my vest had disintegrated, along with everything else I'd stashed in it. I had replacements for most of the things I'd lost, which was a bonus, but had had to resort to packing them in a utility bag until I could commission a new vest to be made.

A utility bag I'd left in the craft.

I had some things on me, but not what I needed. I stood, patting my front two pockets, which were semibulging, to double-check. "I left my bag in the craft. I have to go get it." I'd have to get used to toting that thing around. I needed my stuff to survive. I had time to spare now, but that wouldn't necessarily be the case next time. I had a loop on my pants to hook it to, but it would take some time to get used to wearing it.

Before I could head out, Case reached inside his own pocket. "I may be able to get it open with this." He held a laser key in his hand. It looked similar to a few I had—circular, no bigger than a coin. But his was housed in metal, not the usual lightweight molded poly.

I squatted next to him as he positioned it in front of the lip of the box. Light shot out of the key, and the box began to melt as Case moved the key in small circles, the metal undulating as it was forced by the high temp of the laser to change its physical state. "Holy shit," I exclaimed. "That's a hot laser, not a light laser. I've never seen one that tiny. No wonder it's housed in metal." It was the same technology that made my Gem work, but on a micro level. My Gem was considered a very hot laser. The kind that could sear a gaping hole through you in the blink of an eye. This one's top capability would be burning a pin-sized hole through your finger.

"The only drawback is that it depletes quickly," Case said.

After about ten seconds, it clicked off and he shoved it back in his pocket.

The metal was gooey and had to cool before we could touch it.

"What powers that thing?" I asked. "I've never come across one before."

"A small chemical capacitor," he answered. "The reaction causes the laser to release at a high rate, but

saps after eight to ten seconds. It recharges overnight."
He tentatively placed a finger on the twisted lid, tapping lightly to test the heat.

Then he pried the lid off.

Chapter 5

As Case struggled to get the top off, I contemplated shouldering him out of the way to do it myself. Instead, I reached into my pocket for my ultra-light. It was no bigger than the tip of my finger. I clicked it on, and bright white light flooded the area.

I set it on the nearest box and scanned the rows, counting thirty-one containers, all with the Bliss Corp logo.

One last heave, and the top finally came off with a clatter.

Case panted from the effort as I knelt next to him. We both eagerly glanced inside to see what Bliss Corp had been storing in these lockboxes—containers that someone had taken the time to lug to this remote location to protect. Thirty-one times up and down the slippery, rocky crag. They had to be important.

Aluminum etch boards were stacked to the top.

Before the dark days, they were used in professional

settings, as well as in schools and universities, as note-taking devices. Anything written on the boards was saved to a data chip in the back, later converted into whatever format you needed for easy transfer to your personal computer. They were necessary in a setting where you couldn't use voice transcription, like if a professor was lecturing, or you were in a high-powered Bliss Corp meeting.

Case took one out.

"Turn it over and see if there's a chip," I prompted. He complied, sliding open the seamless compartment on the back.

No data chip.

"Damn," I swore. I was certain the pico had the capacity to read whatever would've been on that chip. "Let's check them all."

While we meticulously went through the stack, Daze walked in. "Are those etch boards?"

"They are," I answered, "but none of them have their chips. Without them, we'll never know what went on in those Bliss Corp meetings." Assuming they were used during meetings—who really knew?

"People stopped using those a long time ago," he said knowingly as he stooped down to pick one up.

"Is that so?" I said, not looking up as I reached for the next board.

"Yeah." He ran his fingers over the polished surface. "Someone invented a tiny voice receiver that transcribed whatever you were listening to word for word, then dumped it into an integrated digital tablet, and all you had to do was touch the screen to highlight what you wanted to keep. It made these things obsolete." He shrugged. "I read about it once when I was a kid."

A kid? "You know, Daze"—I shook my head—"if you're not careful, you're going to reveal how big your brain really is, and after that, there's no going back." I picked up a new etch board, flipping it over. "And here I thought you were just some random street urchin about to terminate himself off a cliff. But in reality, you're a brainiac." I chuckled at the word Cozzi had used to describe Darby. The kid—who was definitely still a kid—might be more than smart, he might be brilliant. Retaining information you'd read only once was an incredible talent and extremely useful in our world, where information was not easily accessible.

But it was too soon to tell him that.

An overinflated ego wouldn't help him in the street-smarts department. You needed a different kind of intelligence to stay alive on the street, and he had a long way to go.

"I'm not that smart. I just remember stuff." *Exactly.* He gave me a shy grin. "My dad was the brainiac."

"Well, he's not the only one." I continued to chuckle as I stood. It was a funny word. I reached up to lift down another box. This one felt lighter. I shook it. Not much noise. These weren't etch boards. "Okay," I said, glancing around. "We're going to have to find another way to unlock the rest of these."

Maisie's muffled voice erupted into the small space. "I detect seven like signatures."

I gave the kid a look. "Is she in your pocket?"

His head bobbed up and down. "Yeah, but I was real careful. I wrapped her in cloth, and I didn't touch the outside. I couldn't keep her in the craft. She's too…"

"Valuable? I get it. Pull her out and ask her what she's talking about," I said. "What are *like* signatures anyway?" I hope that didn't mean there were seven status eggs in here. Although they'd bring in a lot of coin on the market, having them gain their freedom all at once would be a nightmare. We'd have to secure them somewhere *outside* the craft on the way back.

Daze took Maisie out and unwrapped her carefully, while Case set more boxes on the ground so we'd have better access to them. This was going to be a full-scale operation.

"Repeat with more detail," Daze instructed Maisie, holding her so close that his nose was in jeopardy of smudging her. There was a hundred percent chance his breath was fogging up her shell.

A kaleidoscope of light shot around the room, dotting the walls and the containers with tiny specks of light. After a moment, she said, "Computer software detected in the form of artificial intelligence. LiveBot-compatible, not enhanced."

I glanced at Case, hoping he understood the tech jargon better than I did. "Did you get any of that?"

Case shook his head. "Not really. As far as I know, AI technology was the go-to software for all intelligent devices until around the beginning of the twenty-second century. LiveBot software came after, and it was a significant upgrade, because it could learn from its integrated database and from its environment over time. 'Not enhanced' must mean it's not military grade?" He shrugged. "I have no idea."

We both looked to Daze. "Well?" I asked. "Is he close?" I didn't know much either, as there was no need to learn much about AI when it didn't pertain to our world now. AI wasn't going to fix my craft or bring me a protein cake.

"I'm not sure," Daze said, cupping the status reader to his chest. "LiveBot was replacing AI because it was a superior system. The robots acted human. That's all I know."

"Okay." I glanced at the boxes. Salvaging was my specialty. If I couldn't figure out how to open the rest of these, then I should hang up my Gem and call it a day. "According to Maisie, we're looking for something that possibly contains some kind of intelligent software." That sounded promising. "I need to head back to Seven. I have something in my utility bag that should work on opening these up."

I made my way out of the cave quickly, unable to avoid being doused by the rain curtain, and wound my way around the rocks and up the slippery slope, grabbing on to anything that would support my weight. It took only ten minutes, but it felt like an eternity.

Once in the clearing, I spotted Seven, covered in reflective cloth. I was impressed at how well camouflaged she was. I hurried toward her, peeling up the fabric to access the passenger door, only needing to loft it a couple meters. The utility bag was easily accessible, wedged between the two front seats.

After I retrieved it, I slammed the door, dropping the cloth back into place.

A faint *schick-schick* of propellers sounded from above.

They weren't loud enough to be a human-operated dronecraft. I dropped to the ground and rolled under Seven as far as I could before I was stopped by the landing gear. Unmanned aerial crafts, or UACs, weren't common. This one sounded louder than most, which meant it was big, just not big enough to have a pilot. I'd salvaged a military-grade UAC with a working laser a few years ago. We never flew it inside the city limits. If the government found out, they'd confiscate it and I'd be jailed.

The propeller sound intensified.

It had to be over the clearing now. If the thing had a live-video feed, we would be in trouble quickly. But most live-feed units didn't accurately transmit in our iron-particle-clogged world. But I'd know soon enough. If it lingered, someone was checking out the area. If it continued on its way, that likely meant this was a routine stop, and no one would know we were here until it went back to its hub and someone manually downloaded the video to take a look.

That would give us enough time to get out.

Within minutes, the thing passed overhead.

I rolled out from under the craft, sopping wet and covered with mud. I refrained from cursing, knowing I'd need those words once I hit the slope again and took off at a run.

Back in the cave, water sluiced off my shoulders and ran down my arms. I used the momentum to wipe off the dirt and grime as best I could. Case and Daze were back by the guns. "We've got an hour or two, tops," I called as I headed into the tunnel where the boxes were. "A UAC just flew over the clearing. I'm not sure if this is a routine stop, or if the militia is trying to hunt us down. But it was definitely military. Once that thing gets back to the base, there's a high probability whoever is looking is going to notice something. Reflective cloth works well, but it's not infallible."

Case and Daze followed me into the small space. "This is my fault," Case said. "I should've rechecked the data and made sure the flight path was switched on."

"Fault is not at issue here. Finding a safe place for the night is." I glanced around. "But we can't leave without opening these boxes." I set the utility bag down. It was made of durable fiber and had multiple compartments. Before the dark days, people had used these for travel, or so I'd heard. The various sizes and separations made it valuable for carrying the things I needed. I pulled out a universal frequency key. It was roughly the size of my palm and two centimeters thick. It worked by creating a series of random frequencies in a single burst. "Grab the lid off the first one we opened. Let's see once and for all if it's a signal lock or a magnetic one."

Case picked up the lid and inspected the undamaged part of the rim, then picked up the container. "I don't see any mag-strips. But I don't see a signal housing either."

"Give it to me." He handed the box over, and I took off a glove, running a finger around the inside, close to the top. In the corner, my finger bumped over a small groove that contained the frequency mechanism. "It's here, but it's very well made. They must've spent a fortune on these." I tapped the corner on the outside with a fingernail. "The fiber wires run up here and connect with the cover." I traced the inside rim of the lid and found a faint bulge tracking all the way around.

Case's expression showed he was impressed. "How do you know so much about signal locks?"

"I've come across them often enough during my salvaging runs. Finding this handy little helper"—I held up the universal frequency key—"basically changed the way I do business. Things that were out of my reach aren't now."

He crossed his arms, sitting back on his haunches. "But frequency combinations are endless. Those things can combine a max of ten wave combinations at a time. That could take forever."

"That's true." I knelt next to the new box. "But over the years, I've noticed a pattern. Professional lockboxes and larger-frequency safes are too ritzy for their own good. I can almost picture the sales specialist who sold this lot to Bliss Corp." I gestured at the containers. "Touting how superior their locks were, versus the other guy's, because they used an ultrahigh frequency that no one could crack." I programmed the universal key to ultrahigh mixed with a single low pulse. "Most of the locks I've cracked have been ultrahigh with a few low pulses to throw people off. I'm not saying I can break this the first time, but I'm pretty confident the key can figure it out eventually. And as far as time, this key shoots ten billion different combinations into the lock per second." I aimed it at the same corner where I'd found the housing on the other box and depressed the button.

"Who developed the universal keys?" Case asked.

"Hackers."

"Of course."

"From what I've read, hackers lived like royalty. The black market for things like this before the dark days had to have been a trillion-dollar industry. The world was so digitized and dependent on computers, I can't imagine what it cost the average person to protect their personal data." Or what it cost for someone to pay a hacker to break a code.

"It's hard to imagine what that world looked like." The wistfulness in his tone mirrored everyone's when they reflected on all that had been lost.

"Agreed." My finger continuously depressed the button. It'd been running for longer than thirty seconds. I was just about to reposition it and try again when a crack sounded as the edge of the cover popped free.

Daze's impressed whoosh of breath followed by a "cool" behind me was enough to confirm that my salvager instincts had paid off. That, and the prize that waited for us.

I lifted the lid.

Chapter 6

I tried not to be disappointed, but it was seeping in around the edges anyway. I blew out a long breath. The first seven boxes held nothing of note—more etch boards with no data chips, random office supplies, polylaminated folders with nothing in them but sales numbers.

The eighth box was being difficult. I punched the frequency key for the tenth time to try new combinations. This had been the lightest and noisiest box yet. When shifted from the stack, things inside had rolled around, clinking together. The only good thing was that this hadn't taken too much time. We were an hour in.

Case and Daze stared at me with expectant looks. "I'm going as fast as I can," I said. I was well aware that we were going to have to evacuate this place soon—we had an hour, tops, whether or not we got through all the lockboxes.

"There's something different in this one," Case said.

"Yep," I said. "And if they were trying to keep this one extra safe, which seems likely, they might've doubled up on the locks. It might take more than one keyed frequency to get through." I lifted up on the key, switching the dial to half high-frequency, half low-frequency, then depressed the button again.

"Maybe this one is something really different," Daze said. "If all the other ones were ultrahigh, maybe this is all low?"

I shrugged. It was worth a try. While I adjusted the dial once again, I said, "It's too bad Maisie can't just tell us what the frequency is. What good is that egg anyway?" I joked.

Maisie said from inside Daze's pants pocket, "I detect seven—"

"*Like signatures,*" I finished for her. "We know." It was the third time she'd said it in the span of twenty minutes. "Tell us something we don't know."

Maisie replied, "The frequency combination is muted."

I sat up straighter. "Wait, what?" That was new.

Daze's eyes widened. "Something about the frequency being muted."

"The lock frequency? Or another frequency?"

Daze brought the egg up to his mouth. "What frequency are you referring to?"

"The frequency is muted," she repeated in her pleasant cadence.

"Set her next to the box. Maybe proximity matters."

Once Daze settled her on her cloth in front of the box, I leaned over and asked, "Can you decipher the frequency signal three centimeters from you?"

"The frequency combination is muted," she repeated.

"Expand details," I ordered.

"The frequency combination has failed. Locking mechanism will not engage. Suggest using force."

Now we were getting somewhere. "Much better. What kind of force do you have in mind?" I asked. "We're fresh out of hot lasers."

"A solid strike to the signal housing will open it," she said, surprising me. That was specific, and kind of spooky, all in a conversational tone. "I detect seven like signatures inside."

My gaze found Case's. "The like signatures are in this box." Up until this point, Maisie hadn't indicated where the like signatures were located.

Instead of answering, Case turned his attention to the doorway. His pulse gun was out in the next instant. I rose quickly, drawing my Gem. "Daze, get behind me," I ordered as I followed Case out. "What did you hear?" My voice was low.

"It might be nothing," he murmured, moving into the main room. "But it sounded like something landed above us."

Dammit. "If that's true, it took less time than we thought for the UAC to get back to its hub."

"I don't think so," he said. "If it's a dronecraft, we would've heard props. It was something else."

"Something like what?" I asked.

We had our answer in the next moment. Something was in the process of tumbling down the embankment outside the cave. It sounded like metal on stone. I shooed Daze farther into the darkness at the opposite end, away from the opening, while I aimed my gun in front of me.

Case gestured for me to take the left, while he edged right.

We waited. Nothing happened.

No more sounds.

Holding up three fingers, Case stuck his head through the cascading rain. I followed three seconds later. But instead of just my head, I went all the way through, dropping into a low crouch right outside the mouth of the cave. I couldn't see up the hill, because there were large boulders in the way, but I couldn't hear anything other than precipitation hitting my helmet.

Case eased out after me, holding up his entire hand this time, fingers closed. Then he briskly waved it to the left, curving his fingers slightly.

We would move around the corner together.

I nodded to let him know I understood.

He spread his hand wide.

On five, we both sprang, rounding the mouth of the cave, our guns aimed up the hill. I couldn't see anything. Case lowered his hand first. "They sent a bot to check the area," he said, nodding to a small mound stuck between some rocks halfway up the incline.

I finally spotted the object. It was round and matte black, no bigger than the size of Daze's head. "Was it attached to a UAC?" I asked. "I've never seen a bot drop out of the sky before." I squinted. Something was spinning on the bottom. "It looks like it has wheels. Not exactly the right fit for this terrain."

"These are called Charlies," Case said, making his way back. "They're military UACs. Their wings and props contract, and they're 360-degree video-capable. There's a large eye inside the top of the curved dome. They're supposed to be stealthy, almost soundless when they're in the air. The military used them for surveillance before the dark days. If this one hadn't crash-landed, we wouldn't have heard it."

"That thing doesn't look stealthy." I followed Case back inside. "It should be painted a dull gray to fit into our world."

He was already rounding stuff up. "We need to leave now. We exit up the other side, away from the Charlie."

"We can't leave yet," I argued. "We have twenty more boxes to check."

Case shook his head. "No. We head out now, and when the militia is not tracking us, we come back."

I sighed. He was right. That was happening a lot more lately, and I wasn't sure how I felt about it. If the militia had sent out this Charlie, they had more than an inkling we were in this area. It was time to move.

Heading into the tunnel, I grabbed my utility bag off the ground, stuffing the frequency key and my ultra-light inside, attaching it to a loop at my waist. I picked up the lockbox we'd been trying to get open and tucked it under my arm. I came out to find Daze with his pack on, the smallest laser gun he'd found in the container in his fist. It looked gigantic.

Before I could tell him that there was no way in hell he was bringing it with us, he held up his hand in the universal gesture of *wait until I've explained myself before you say no.* "It doesn't work. There is no fuel cell. I triple-checked. Can I please keep it? Bender might be able to fix it for me. I promise I won't use it until I'm trained."

"I thought Bender already gave you a laser gun," I said.

"That was only to borrow," Daze replied solemnly. Then he perked up. "This counts as my first real salvage." He gave me an imploring look that was pretty damn effective. "I'll always remember it." The kid had a point. I would never forget my first find. It was a pixie motor. I still had it.

"Fine, but once we get back in the craft, stash it somewhere safe," I told him. "We're leaving now. We'll circle back here on the return trip to the city, if we can lose the militia." Case wasn't inside the cave, so I assumed he'd gone to scan the area or headed to Seven to get her ready to go. I grabbed my pack on the way out, slinging it over my shoulder. "Come on, let's go."

The other side of the hill was just as rocky and hard to maneuver as the first side I'd gone up. The contents of the box rattled around under my arm. They certainly weren't etch boards. The kid slipped and slid until I grabbed him by the elbow and tugged him up behind me. He weighed almost nothing. No wonder he couldn't get any traction.

We hurried across the field. The reflective cloth covering Seven was gone, and she was stabilized a meter off the ground.

Case was ready to go.

His intensity about the situation made me uneasy. He knew the militia better than I did, and judging by his reactions, they were more than just a dangerous threat.

Once I was in the passenger side and strapped in, I turned to him. "What's the plan?"

He took us into the air, wasting no time, gaining altitude faster than he had in the past.

He grunted. "Get as far away as possible."

"Why don't these guys just go to the city? It's only four hours away. They obviously have means. Why not join regular civilization?" I knew the answer to that question as soon as the words left my mouth. They were outskirts and would always be outskirts. Following somebody else's laws and keeping within the rules and confines of the city would be impossible. For all intents and purposes, these guys were rogues. They'd been living that way their entire lives. They weren't above stealing, killing, and pillaging to get what they needed.

In fact, they enjoyed it.

Case gave me a look. "They are way past assimilation."

The rain lessened a bit. I glanced out the window, trying to spot anything in the distance that might or might not be following us. "Ask Maisie if there is anything out there," I told Daze as I kept my focus on the sky to my right.

Before Daze could relay the question, Maisie said, "Using my name, Maisie, before a question will elicit a response when uttered at a decibel level of ten or higher. There are no piloted crafts in the area. I detect one UAC five kilometers to the west."

Maisie was indeed learning, and it was slightly unnerving. "That's not what I wanted to hear," I muttered. A UAC still in the area was a problem.

"The correct response is not always optimal," Maisie agreed.

"I didn't utter your name, Maisie," I replied. "I thought that was the prompt."

"We are engaged in a conversation. To end it, simply say, 'Stop.'"

"Stop," I said as I turned to Case, not having time to engage with the egg. "The UAC is likely the one I saw in the clearing doing its rounds. At least we know it hasn't gone back to its base yet. That's something." Case veered the craft east, or what I thought was east. Our radar and radio were still off, just to be safe. "The UAC won't be able to catch up with us, right?" I asked. "It can't go as fast as Seven. Are you thinking about activating another hydro-boost?"

"This craft is only set for one at a time," Case replied. "I didn't load another one when we landed, which was a mistake."

"Yeah, forgetting stuff like that could get us killed," I said, turning to do a full grid scan out my passenger window. We were flying over some rolling hills, dead like everything else, but there were ample places to set down. "You could land down there and add another boost."

He shook his head. "We'll be over the ocean in less than ten minutes, by my calculations," he said. "They won't pursue us there. The chance of losing the UAC is too great. It will be programmed to turn back before it hits the sea."

I turned to him, suddenly alarmed. "Can't we just hug the coast? And if we see the UAC, then go over the ocean?"

Case had the nerve to chuckle, knowing how much I hated flying over the roiling sea. The waves were massive and angry, kicking up torrents of turbulent air. It was heart-stopping. "If we want to make sure we stay in the clear, which we do, the ocean is the only option."

I crossed my arms. "My totally sensible idea about landing and putting in another boost is much better. You know I hate the sea. It's vicious and unforgiving."

He gave me a sideways glance. "And where exactly do you think we're going to find the sodium alginate?"

Chapter 7

I startled awake. It was dark, and everything was quiet. Case wasn't in the pilot's seat. I whipped my head around, relieved to see Daze sprawled in the back, snoring lightly. I ran a hand over my face, reaching for my helmet.

My first thought was that Case had drugged me again.

On a good day, I was a light sleeper. The ocean had been terrifying, and we'd been over it a long time, then I didn't remember a thing.

"Dammit," I muttered as I donned my headgear and drew my Gem, easing the door open. "Never trust someone who's played you not once, but twice. What was his plan anyway? To dump us in the middle of nowhere and leave us to rot?"

"Not exactly," Case answered, surprising me. It was much too close, especially since I couldn't see him. "And I didn't drug you."

"I didn't say you did." *Not exactly anyway.* I was fully out of the craft now, glancing around. I still couldn't see him.

"Sometimes the body gives out during a stress response," he continued. "I've seen it many times."

His voice was coming from underneath the craft. I flipped on a shoulder light and bent down. "I wasn't stressed." In fact, I'd been hyperstressed. My body actually felt sore from all the muscle tightness.

In the city, there was a predictable kind of danger, one I met head on daily. Out here was something new and wild. The instability of it all had me rattled, more than I'd like to admit—I certainly wasn't admitting it to the outskirt.

Case rolled out, holding a spent hydrogen container, and I took a step back.

He stood, brushing the muck from his sleeves. "You can kid yourself all you want," he said. "But you hyperventilated for at least five minutes before you passed out. How much sleep did you get last night?"

"None." I was done talking about this. As long as Case hadn't drugged me, and we weren't in the hands of the militia, I was good. I turned in a circle. "Where are we?"

"Right outside the boundary of my town in an area I like to call Hidden Cove. It's protected on all sides and hard to get to without a craft. We're protected here for at least the night."

"Does the militia extend this far?" I asked. "Are they going to continue pursuing us?"

"If they recognized my craft, yes," he said.

"Seven used to be Dixon's, right?" He gave me an infinitesimal nod. "They wouldn't have recognized Luce." I climbed back into the craft to get out of the rain, letting that sit for a while. He'd argued about taking Seven, but he had to have known there was a chance the militia would scout us at some point.

Case got in the other side. "If I'd thought there was a chance they'd see us, I would've insisted on taking your craft."

I didn't know if I should believe him or not. He was as stubborn as I was when it came to admitting fault. I was too fatigued to dwell on it. I rested my head against the seat, pulling off my helmet, the blue light from my shoulder illuminating the small space between us. "Do you think your siblings will talk tomorrow?"

"If they don't, I plan to make them."

"You know, there's a chance the militia has taken over your tribe since Tandor left," I said. "By taking most of the residents with him, Tandor weakened their resistance to fight back. It would be easy for the militia to force the remaining inhabitants to assimilate if there were only a few left." I peeled off a glove and ran a hand over my face. "I wouldn't rule out that Tandor knew this and may have even brokered a deal with them. After all, he wanted to be the supreme ruler of the city, and if he had the aid and cooperation of the biggest militia in the South behind him, by handing them tribes to rule, he might've been invincible." I shuddered to think about what that world would've looked like. Widespread panic, violence, and chaos. The majority of the human race wouldn't have made it through a year.

Case nodded, taking his helmet off and resting his own head on the seat back. We were both beat. "That seems like a likely reality. Given how much effort the militia is taking to pursue us, it seems that in a very short amount of time they've gained even more power. It's not something I'd considered, but should have. Honestly, I never thought Tandor would be successful, and I certainly didn't think he had planned anything more than whipping a few people into a frenzy in a halfhearted attempt to take over the government. He was dangerous and cruel, but lacked any sort of follow-through, which his followers, including Hutch, knew. It's looking like he was more devious than I gave him credit for."

"I only made his acquaintance once for a short time, but I underestimated him as well," I said. "He was sloppy about the planning, but apparently not about the implementation." Wishing Case had known more about what we were getting into down here was wishful thinking. When he'd followed Tandor to the city, it'd been fueled by revenge and a highly emotional response to his nephew being violently murdered. Not thinking straight was a given. "How far out of town are we?"

"Around three kilometers."

"That's fairly close," I said, pondering the situation

for a moment. "I think it makes sense if I go in and question your siblings alone. If we can prevent the militia from finding out that you're connected to this craft, maybe they'll give up trying to find us. I'm an unknown around here. A strange woman looking for supplies. Not a threat. If the militia comes to town after we've left, your siblings describe me and not you. They won't even know you were here."

"That might work, but my sustainee brother is a—"

Case was interrupted by a semimuffled, silky female voice coming from the backseat, likely clutched in Daze's hand. "I detect three humans and seven like signatures within three meters," Maisie said. "Female, Holly, blood pressure normal, heart rate optimal, nutrition inadequate. Recommend hydration."

"Why does she only care about my stats?" I grumbled. But the egg had just reminded us that we still hadn't opened the box with the mysterious *like signatures*. I plucked it up from where it sat near my feet, wondering if Maisie had interrupted us because she wanted us to find out what was inside. "Do you think your laser key is charged enough to get this thing open? Since the frequency signature is broken, the only way to get it open is with force. The key should work."

He reached into his pocket and pulled it out. "It might not have a full charge, but a few seconds should be sufficient."

I angled the box toward Case, anxious to see what was inside. Aiming the key at the corner, where the housing was, he depressed the button. If the connection mechanism was destroyed, it would open.

The hot laser ran for four seconds, but the metal was twisted and molten. After about thirty seconds, I tested it with my finger. It was cool enough to the touch, so I tucked the box under my arm and tried to pry the lid off, using my body as leverage.

It wouldn't budge.

Case reached out a hand, and I gave it to him. He braced it between his legs and pulled, the cover wrenching upward almost instantaneously. He chuckled. "It wouldn't have opened unless you loosened it for me first." As he lifted the box up, four out of seven small silver cylindrical items tumbled into his lap.

I reached over and picked one up, turning it over in my hand. Case set the box with the rest of them on the floor.

We needed more light, so I took out my ultra-light, and the entire inside of the craft lit up.

Daze sat up in the backseat, rubbing his eyes, instantly alert when he saw what we were doing. "Whoa, are those bullets?"

"No," I said. At least, I didn't think they were. "They certainly look like they could be. They're the right shape. But they're too light and too well made. They've been polished to a high sheen. Nobody would spend that much time and money on a bullet." They were smooth all over, with no discernible markings. Lead bullets hadn't been around for over a century, but some guns used specific kinds of ammunition. Like Lockland's Blaster. Those bullets were bigger than these and filled with scrap metal.

"I detect seven like signatures," Maisie repeated.

"We know," I muttered. "And we're currently trying to figure out what they are. It would be extremely helpful if you could identify them for us instead of calling them 'like signatures.' If not, feel free to take a breather."

"My technological composition does not require oxygen to function," she answered.

I snorted as Daze laughed. "Duly noted," I said. "But that's not the question I was hoping you'd answer. What are these things?" Just for the hell of it, I placed one in front of the egg that Daze was now holding between the seats. "Come on, Maisie. You can do it. What are these things?"

Her lights blinked away, and I got hopeful she was going to solve the mystery. "I detect seven like signatures in the form of artificial intelligence, LiveBot-compatible, but not enhanced."

"Yes, yes, we know," I said, frustration rising. "That's what's inside, but what are these things? They can't be bullets. For one, they're not heavy enough."

Case examined the one in his hand, and Daze reached for another.

Maisie was quiet for a moment, before saying, "Outer shell made of hyperalloyed aluminum. Interior made of silica and silicon diodes."

"Better," I said. "But that still doesn't tell us what

they are or what they were used for." If they contained *like signatures*, they had to have software inside. But how did they open? What were they used for?

"I think I've seen these before," Daze said.

"They do look familiar," I agreed. "But my brain is being about as helpful as Maisie. Hopefully, your awesome memory will kick in soon."

A pop sounded.

I glanced over at Case, who was now holding one end of the silver bullet in one hand, the cap in the other.

The thing opened. Now we were getting somewhere.

Chapter 8

"What is it?" I asked. "The suspense is killing me." We all moved closer to get a better look. Case held up the exposed end, setting the sleek, cylindrical cap in his lap. He brought the shell to his nose and took a sniff. I wrinkled my nose. "Does it smell?"

"Not really," he answered. "I was just checking to see if it had any chemical makeup I could detect." He rolled it back and forth between his fingers. A small glint inside caught the light. He brought it closer, squinting. "I think there's a mirror of some kind inside."

"A mirror?" I squinted, trying to see the tiny reflection.

"Can I look?" Daze asked. He set Maisie on the console between us as Case handed him the confusing trinket. Daze began twisting the bottom. On the second rotation, light flickered from the inside. On consecutive turns, it went from blue, to green, to purple. He held it closer to his face, and the light hit his iris, making it reflect purple for a brief instant.

I gasped, finally understanding. "I know what that is! It's a diffraction grater."

"A what?" Case asked, picking up another one and taking off the cap.

"It's what our ancestors used to change their eye color temporarily." I popped one open, examining it. "Through laser sculpting, they could alter the surface of the cornea, cutting ridges to absorb the color they wanted, reflecting everything else. But it only lasted a week at the most. As the eye healed, it went back to normal." Sounded painful to me. I shook the thing. "These could've been some kind of promotional tools Bliss Corp gave away." It was hard not to be disappointed. "I'm not sure what Maisie was talking about with the AI, but it must take some software to run these. Who knows?" I turned it over and tried to pry the bottom off. There was no seam to indicate it could be opened.

Case studied his. "I've heard about these things. Weren't they called something like Eye Dids?"

I chuckled. "I think they were called Eye Diffs for short. The technical term for the process was eye diffraction." I put the cap back on, turning it over in my hand. "What I don't understand is why anyone would want to use one. Realigning the tissue means damaging it. The risk of going blind had to be high. But I guess it makes sense that Bliss Corp would have them."

He shrugged, sitting back. "The beauty industry was big business."

"Yeah, second only to the pleasure industry," I said. "Bliss Corp carried a line of high-quality beauty products." I shook the bullet-shaped object. "If you didn't have money to pay for permanent alterations, you settled for temporary fixes. From what I've read, which isn't much, most of the gene pool had become homologized eighty to a hundred years ago, and unless your parents decided to go with gene editing before you were born, which was only available to the wealthy, you looked like everyone else. Things like these"—I held up the diffractor—"made you stand out."

"I think it's cool. It couldn't have hurt that much, or people wouldn't have done it," Daze said. "Can I try it?"

I plucked the thing out of his grasp before he had a chance to place it near his eye. "Let's not mess around with your vision. Sight is a beautiful thing." The gadgets had probably been sitting around for over sixty years. "I wouldn't trust the technology anymore either." I gathered up the rest of the Eye Diffs, picking the other three out of the container, and opened a dash compartment and tumbled them inside. "Well, that's disappointing." I wasn't sure what secrets I'd thought we'd uncover from Bliss Corp, but old beauty products hadn't made the list. "I refuse to give up hope. There are still some boxes in the cave." There was a reason someone thought it was important to store them out of reach of human interference. "But we can't do anything now except get some sleep. I say we set out in a few hours, just before dawn. It will be better to take them by surprise, before the day starts."

"I'm not tired," Daze said.

"You were snoring ten minutes ago. I'm pretty sure you can find your groove again pretty quickly," I replied.

"I'm hungry," he said.

On cue, my stomach gave a loud gurgle, and Maisie responded with, "Nutrient deficiency detected in all three humans—one adult male, one male child, one adult female, also known as Holly. Intake of essential aminos and calories necessary. Recommend hydration. UV exposure critical."

"No sun lamps until we're home, so UV is out. The child is Daze, and the adult male is Case," I told Maisie. "No need to single me out. You can go ahead and talk about their deficiencies just as much as mine." I couldn't help grumbling, having no idea if she was learning from my words or not. I turned to Daze. "You heard the egg. Let's eat." I was still worried about Daze's health. I should've been forcing him to eat more frequently, but there'd been too much stuff going on. I reached for my pack, which I'd placed on the floor behind my seat. Actually, I'd rocketed it back there without much thought. Daze had situated it on the floor. I asked Case, "Do you have a jug of water nearby?" Which was code for, *Will you please get us some water?*

Case got out and walked around the back, popped the storage compartment, and brought back a jug. I pulled a cup out of my pack and held it out. Case filled it with water. Then I plunged the ultrasonic whisk inside and turned it on.

The water was bubbling in ten seconds.

Eating cold slop was a drag, so it was lucky these whisks were small and easy to travel with. They'd been invented by some guy trying to make an integrated ultrasonic scrubber for a newly designed bio-toilet. Apparently, the toilet water started boiling.

Daze held out three packages of dried food. I added water straight to the bags.

Instant protein mush. We ate in silence.

I wasn't certain what my meal flavor was supposed to be, but it was fairly tasty. These rations had been made before the dark days. They tasted different than the protein cakes the government made with their 3-D bio-printers, and honestly, it was a relief to taste something different. I couldn't imagine all the choices our ancestors had at their fingertips before disaster had wreaked its havoc. It must've been hard to constantly have to make decisions about what to eat.

It was a life I'd never know.

I finished the last few bites and contemplated having another bag. We'd packed at least a month's worth, even though we'd planned on being out for only a couple of days. Traveling this far in an average craft was difficult. Keeping your batteries charged was an issue. You had to have spares. We were incredibly lucky that the barracks had a room full of super-powerful batteries, and because of that, we had more than enough battery power to stay out here for a couple months, if need be. So why not bring enough food? That way, if we ran into trouble, we'd be covered.

I decided against another meal. I was full, regardless of what Maisie thought of my nutrient level. We discarded the empty packages into a bio-bag we would grind up later. I yawned, settling back against the seat. "I suggest you get some sleep, even if you're not tired," I told Daze. "We're leaving just before dawn, and it's going to be a long walk."

"Fine," Daze said. "But I'm probably not going to fall asleep. When I'm not tired, there's nothing I can do to get to sleep. It just doesn't happen."

The kid was snoring six minutes later.

It took me an additional ten to join him.

It was dark when we set out, the sun set to rise within the hour. In the city, even during blackout, it seemed like there was a bit of ambient light. Out here, with nothing around, the darkness was complete, settling over my body like a second skin. We had our shoulder lights on so we could see. The deep blue light wouldn't be detected at a distance very easily.

Before we'd left the city, I'd found a decent jacket for Daze in one of my caches and managed to incorporate a single shoulder light with a little bit of polygel adhesive. The lights came in red, blue, and green, were fairly abundant, and ran on a tiny nano-helium battery. Without batteries, life wouldn't be remotely possible.

When I thought about it, I always tried to remember to give thanks to the guy who'd invented the long-lasting helium batteries right before the dark days. He was our true savior, even though his name hadn't been recorded.

Some things had just been lost forever.

I sidestepped a large rock. I'd tripped three times already, so I was hyperaware. We'd trudged up and down several muddy, wet hills. "Are you sure you know where you're going?" I asked Case for the third time. "I could swear we're going in circles."

He was a good four meters in front of me. "Not exactly, but close enough."

That version of the facts was a little different than the one he'd given me three minutes ago. Three minutes ago, he'd been positive we were heading in the right direction. "If we didn't have Maisie, I'd be worried," I quipped. "Trying to retrace our steps coming back in this landscape wouldn't be fun." The earth beneath our feet was a mixture of sand, dirt, and dead vegetation mixed with water. It was a soggy mess.

"I've walked in this way before," he said. "No matter which way I veer, it leads to town. I'm just not sure which part of town we'll end up in."

Daze trudged behind me, not complaining. The kid definitely had guts. When I'd woken him up, he'd been raring to go. I wasn't going to lie, I'd felt a little trepidation about bringing him along. But leaving him in Seven for who knew how long, when the militia was likely after us, hadn't been a good idea either. It was best to have him close.

"Let's go over the plan again," I said, quickening my steps to come even with Case. "You think your sustainee sister Wendra is the better bet. Your sustainee brother Freedom is a handful, but might know something." What kind of a name was Freedom anyway? I had no ground to stand on, with a name like Hollywood California. Names ran the gamut around here. In fact, I knew somebody named Gamut. "Do they live near each other?"

"Not exactly," he answered, his voice tight. "They live on opposite ends of town. They don't like each other much."

"You said Wendra's residence has neighbors, but that Freedom lives more remotely and in a bigger group."

"That's correct."

"What do you mean by bigger group?"

"He has a lot of wives."

Wives?

It was extremely old-fashioned to have even *one* wife. Nobody bothered with ceremonies anymore. No one cared that much. You sort of paired up, and that was the end of it.

"That's…odd," I settled on.

"My sustainer parents were Sun Optimists. They did things the old way. There was a lot of praying and honoring past rituals. Most of my siblings continue to do that."

"Okay, then I find Freedom first," I said. Made sense to me. "Since he's in a more remote location, that works better."

"Yeah, but Wendra is known for having good information," he countered. "If there's gossip about Tandor, she'll have it. It's early enough, depending on where we come in, we can probably get her alone before the others wake up."

"*I'm* the one that's going to get to her, not you. We've already been over this, Case. The militia doesn't know about me." Yet. "We don't want you linked to Seven. There's a greater likelihood they'll decide to back off if you're not in the picture. A lone woman is much less of a threat."

"I'm not sure what you're going to get. Tribes are very close-knit, and they don't like outsiders."

I glanced back to make sure Daze was still behind us. He was, but the excitement in his step had dwindled. "Are you doubting my abilities to get someone to talk? And I never mentioned it would be easy. I just know my way around these things. Gaining information is my specialty." First, I asked nice, then I didn't.

Case was quiet for more than a minute. When he spoke next, I had to strain to hear him. "I killed a few people before I left, so it's best if you go in alone. I won't be welcome here."

I shook my head slowly. He couldn't see me, because he was a few steps ahead, but my tone took care of the rest. "And you left that out of our previous discussions, *why?*"

"Because it doesn't matter," he said. "We would've come here even if I hadn't killed anyone. We need to find the sodium alginate, and to do that we have to figure out where Tandor came from. That's our mission. What I did before doesn't matter."

"It certainly does," I retorted. "How your siblings will react to seeing you, even before the militia factored in, is pertinent information. It affects the plan. Running into a little bit of trouble with your tribe doesn't equal getting killed the moment we step foot into town because you blew people up and didn't tell me."

"I didn't blow them up."

I was about to tell him exactly what I thought of his glaring omission when Daze hurried forward and cut in with, "Who'd you kill?"

"I killed two of my sustainee siblings," Case muttered, clearly not wanting to discuss the matter.

Yeah, Case not being welcome here *was an understatement.*

"Why'd you do that?" Daze asked. The kid's tone had turned contemplative. Killing family was a big deal.

He knew it, I knew it, Case knew it.

"Because they helped kill Frankie."

Chapter 9

Frankie had been Case's nephew, the son of Carmen, his sustainee sister who died along with Tandor and most of his crew on the gorge that day. Frankie was the reason Case had come to the city, why he'd followed Tandor, and why he'd wanted his revenge.

Daze didn't know most of that, and when Case didn't offer up any details, I filled in what I knew. "Frankie was Case's nephew. He was killed on Tandor's orders." I left out that he'd been killed by his mother and, it now appeared, some others.

"You killed some adults for hurting a kid?" Daze asked Case, awe in his tone. In Daze's world, kids were disposable. Nothing more than irritations.

"I did," Case said tightly. "I have no regrets. They deserved to die."

I suspected they did, as Case had told me that Frankie's death had been horrible. "In light of this new information," I said, coming to a stop, "I think you two should stay here and let me go the rest of the way alone. Not only do we have to worry about the militia finding out you were here," I said to Case, who was still walking, "but there's no need for your siblings to know either."

"That's not going to happen," Case said, calling over his shoulder, not slowing.

The sky was beginning to lighten incrementally, an indication that the sun we couldn't see was about to crest over the horizon. I caught up with him, grabbing his arm to pull him to a stop. He was being stubborn, but I wasn't taking no for an answer. "Listen, things have changed now that I have most of the facts"—I wasn't going to pretend that I had them all, because Case was cagey like that—"and we need to formulate an appropriate plan, which includes you staying clear of anyone who would recognize you. If you murdered your siblings, and the family remains close, they aren't going to negotiate with you—they're going to kill you—and us, if we're with you. On sight. I go in, extract the necessary information however I can, and we're out of here. That's the only way this is going to work."

He looked like he was going to argue, but instead focused his gaze over my shoulder. "Fine," he said through an extremely tight jaw. "But the kid and I stay close enough to be on hand if any danger arises, which is at least another kilometer."

"My only requirement is that you stay out of sight." I drew a tech phone out of my pocket. Lockland had given a phone to Case yesterday morning. I turned the dial. "We can use these. There's a way to keep the channel open, but the volume has to be almost all the way down or the static comes through." Case brought his phone out. I took it from him and set the dials to the same frequency. There wasn't a radio receiver here, as far as I knew, but I wasn't interested in talking over the channels. We just needed this to operate as a two-way communication device. A mic chip would've worked better, but I'd lost my earpiece to Dill and the radium ball and didn't have a spare. I gave the phone back to Case. "We have to be within sixty meters for them to work accurately, which won't be a problem," I said. "Basically, while mine's on, you'll hear every word I'm saying. If I need you, I'll let you know."

"I have one, too," Daze said as he pulled out the tech phone Lockland had given him before Tandor had kidnapped him outside his residence. I hadn't known he still had it. I took it from him and set it to the same channel. Then I handed it back.

"Be careful not to let anyone hear the static. Keep it in your pocket," I told him. "It might be better if you and Case split up. That way we can cover ourselves better. Did you bring your taser with you?" Daze grinned as he lifted up his shirt to show me that it was strapped to his waistband. It was smaller than the laser gun he'd taken from the cave, but not by much. "Set it to most pain inflicted," I told him.

"It's not a full tase, it's just half," he replied glumly. Tasers were made with varying amperage. The one I carried could stop a heart if it was set at high. It was called a full tase, or just a taser. Daze's put out less amperage, and its official name was a stunner, since it only had the capacity to stun. But most referred to it as a half tase.

I bent over to whisper in his ear, "I'll let you in on a secret. You can make yours more powerful by not letting up on the trigger. Bender rigged this one so it has a longer continuous burst. As long as your finger stays connected to the trigger, it continues emitting current." I wasn't going to tell the kid that Bender had given him a half tase because he thought he might hurt himself. Instead, I was going to build it up as a secret weapon, which it kind of was.

I was an emotional architect like that.

The kid withdrew it, turning it over in his hand, looking back at me, his skepticism showing. "Really?"

"Really," I said. "It's a badass weapon. If you have your tech phone on and you hear me call for help, have that thing ready to go." I didn't stick around to see his expression change to wonder. I was already moving.

We walked the remaining one and a half kilometers in silence. The sky brightened with each step. It was always hard to tell what was going on with all the cloud cover. I'd wanted to hit the town right at dawn, so our timing was pretty much on target.

We rounded the top of a short hill, and Case came to an abrupt stop. I followed, taking his cue. He was tense.

The sound hit my ears a second later.

Props.

Shit.

Maisie followed with, "I detect an incoming craft, eleven kilometers and closing."

The militia was going to make our trip here harder than it had to be, assuming it was the militia.

"Are there a lot of crafts in the tribe?" I asked Case.

He shook his head. "Not a one."

"Damn. I have to get to town before they land," I said, starting to jog. I took in the landscape around us. It was similar to what we'd traversed all morning, but in front of us more dead trees had begun to spring up, and the landscape was noticeably less hilly. Case and Daze followed me. "Can you tell whose house we're closest to now?" I asked Case. "Does the area look familiar?"

"We're closest to Freedom's," he said as he gestured to the right. "If you continue around that bend, you'll see it. It's nothing more than an oversized shack made of reclaimed steel and graphene. Many of the tribe members live underground, or partially underground, but Freedom prefers above ground." He muttered, "He never did well below."

"Got it," I said, slowing to a stop. "This shouldn't take too long." It was a bummer we weren't near Wendra's, but by the sound of the props, we picked the better end of town to come into.

Case grunted. "Freedom is…peculiar."

I glanced over. "Peculiar? In what way?" If I was

going to do this job, I needed as much information as I could get.

"He was struck by falling debris when he was a child," Case said as both of us waited for Daze to catch up. "It's made him unstable."

"Unstable, as in violent?"

"Sometimes."

"If I knock on the door, will he come out and talk to me alone?" I asked.

"Not likely," Case said. "You're going to have to be more forceful to get his attention. His wives and children will be inside, but he won't let you talk to them."

Children? Damn. I drew out my Gem. "So, you're telling me I'm on my way to deal with an unstable man with a tendency for violence with a houseful of women and children?" I wasn't going to state the obvious, that these details would've been helpful to have before now. I rechecked my Gem to make sure it was full of nano-carbon cubes. I snapped the cap back into place, put it back in my belt, and drew out my taser. "Don't answer that. I know what to do." I glanced at Daze, who was bent over, hands on his knees and wheezing from the effort of running. "You and Case stay back here while I go in. I'll alert you if there's an issue." I took off, not waiting for either of them to respond, sticking to the trees and bushes lining the hill as best I could.

As soon as I came around the corner, I saw the wobbly shack. Case hadn't been kidding. It was fairly large, but made of nothing more than a bunch of rickety metal pieces welded together. I scanned the sky. The props had gotten louder, but I couldn't see anything overhead from this vantage point.

I crept forward, a bunch of different options about how to get Freedom to cooperate pinging around in my brain. I could knock and hope for the best. I could kick the door in and take everyone by surprise. Or I could knock loudly, then step out of sight until Freedom came out to see what all the ruckus was about. That would effectively get him away from his wives and children. The last thing I wanted was for innocents to get hurt if the situation with this unstable guy spiraled out of control.

With the props getting closer, I had to move.

I chose option number three.

Once at the front door, I wasn't entirely sure that knocking wouldn't make the entire shack collapse, but I took my chances. I rapped the butt of my taser against the flimsy metal. It sounded like a macro-sledge echoing on a steel drum.

Then I vanished around the corner.

The structure didn't have a single window, so I wasn't worried about being seen. My plan was to stay put until Freedom came looking.

"Who the fuck is there?" a loud male voice boomed. It was deeper than I'd anticipated. When I didn't reveal myself, he called again, "Tell me who's out there or I'll separate your head from off your body!" A child began to cry. Not the response I'd hoped for. Who didn't answer their door? How many visitors could this guy have at daybreak? My guess was zero. Zero visitors. This should warrant some action on his part. Couldn't he hear the props?

A woman's voice soothed the crying kid in hushed tones. The walls—that weren't really walls—were painfully thin. I could hear everything.

There was movement inside, but nobody opened the front door.

I sighed.

I was just about to make my way back to the front door to do it all over again, when a tiny voice came through a crack next to me.

"Who are you?" The voice was almost too quiet for me to hear.

I dropped down to a crouch, finding the seam, and was greeted by the eyeball of a small child. My best guess was the kid was no more than three or four years old. "I came to see your daddy," I whispered as softly as I could. "Is he in there?" Instead of the kid answering, the eyeball moved up and down. "Can you make him come out and talk to me?" The props were getting louder by the moment. I glanced upward, but still couldn't see a craft. I was running out of time.

The eye shifted side to side, then got wider. I could see white all the way around. The kid was petrified of his or her father. Poor thing.

"Sampson, who you talking to?" an angry male voice screamed as the kid was violently dragged away. I stood, easing around the back corner of the house soundlessly. "I said, who you talking to?" There was a loud smack, and the child screamed.

It was a blood-curdling sound.

Freedom hadn't just hit the kid, he'd pounded him. I knew firsthand how that felt. Though I'd been eight, not four, the first time I'd been struck like that.

Enough.

Freedom was more than violent—he was a fucking psychopath who didn't hesitate to hurt a child. The only way I was getting the information I needed was by force. And teaching this asshole a lesson in humanity had just jumped to number one on my to-do list.

I took out my Gem, keeping my taser in my left hand, and dragged both weapons along the back of the house as I ran, drumming them as loudly as I could, yelling, "It's me, you son of a bitch! Come out and play!" The only language this guy understood was violence.

I could adjust, no problem.

A shot exploded through the back wall, and shards of broken metal and debris sailed into the dead trees lined up behind the residence. It'd been pure luck that I hadn't been standing in that particular place.

Freedom had a Blaster. The same weapon Lockland used.

It was a dangerous fucking gun to have with all those little kids around, and I was looking forward to remedying that situation for him.

I circled around to the front and kicked in the door, because it was the last place he'd be looking for me. True to my assumption, he was facing the back wall, gun raised, waiting for me to goad him again.

I tackled him before he had a chance to turn around, tasing him in the neck as my elbow locked around his throat. As he fell, I braced his body against my chest, my knee jammed into his spine, forcing his legs to buckle and keep holding some of his weight.

Once I knew he was down, for at least the next several minutes, I glanced around the pitiful scene that was the inside of the house—*house* was a loose term. The place was a rathole. Dirt floors, broken furniture, trash strewn around. The only available light shone through several gaping cracks in the ceiling, along with a constant stream of drizzle. The stale scent of garbage and mildew wafted up my nose.

Three women stood facing me, each one in a corner. They had shoved various children behind them, stark fear on their faces.

"I'm not here to hurt anyone," I told them. "Except this asshole." I shook Freedom hard enough for his head to bob around. "I'm here for information, and that's it." I watched each of their faces, looking for a perceptible facial change that would indicate who I was dealing with. I saw it in the woman who had the most children behind her. After a moment, she took a step forward. I was going to make this easy on her, so I preempted with, "Do you want him to keep breathing?" When she didn't readily answer, I asked, "I need a yes or no. He won't know either way." Very slowly, she nodded yes, but I could see the hesitation in her eyes. He must provide them with *something* that would warrant his continued existence. I inclined my head, so she'd know I'd heard her. Then I reached down and holstered my Gem and withdrew a knife I had concealed at my waist. Dragging Freedom with me, his legs bumping over the dirty floor, I walked over and set the blade in her hand. "This is for you. He won't know you have it. Use it when you need it and don't look back. Do you understand?"

Her fingers curled around the carbon handle as she nodded.

I continued dragging Freedom out the front door. As I left, I saw her rush to the back wall and start digging a hole. I had a feeling she'd use the blade sooner rather than later.

Once I was outside, I hefted Freedom toward the side of the house to keep out of sight of the road, where I planned to continue my chat with him when he awoke.

As I turned the corner, I almost smacked into Case, Daze just behind him. "What the hell are you two doing here?" I dumped Freedom on the ground, where he immediately started to groan. He'd come around in another thirty seconds or so.

Case stared at me blankly, then down at his sustainee brother. "I heard the shot and we decided to come. I thought..."

"You thought wrong." I crouched by Freedom, wresting the Blaster out of his hand. His grip on it was impressive. I held the weapon out to Daze. "As long as you're here, take this and get rid of it. Handle it carefully. Bury it somewhere he won't find it. Go now."

Daze did as I asked as I checked the rest of Freedom's pockets. They were clear. I stood, facing Case, who still had the same blank look on his face. "An SOS from me is when I actually say S-O-S, and most of the time I'll swear. If you don't hear me call explicitly for help, don't come running. But now that you're here, be useful and help me tie this creep up." The prop noise was at maximum. The craft was landing nearby. "By my count, we have five minutes, max." I placed my hands on my hips. "And you undersold your brother's level of crazy. He's not unstable, he's a stone-cold psychopath."

Chapter 10

Freedom came to with a bellow of rage. I'd expected nothing less. Case and I had tied him up with my miracle cord, which I always had with me, vest or not. But for the first time ever, I wasn't sure it was going to hold.

If he managed to break my magic rope, he was going to feel some serious pain. I loved that stuff.

He thrashed around until I squatted next to him, settling my Gem against his temple. The top of his head didn't have a single speck of hair and was dipped in on one side. I guess Case's explanation of falling debris in this situation meant a skull deformity. It actually explained a lot.

I got up close and personal. "All we need you to do is answer a few questions. Then we'll disappear. No harm done," I said. I wasn't going to leave him conscious, but he didn't have to know that right up front. "You remember your brother here, don't you?"

When he didn't even pretend to look in Case's direction, I forced his battered cranium to the side with the tip of my weapon. Stubborn bastard.

Freedom began to thrash once his eyes landed on Case. "You son of a bitch! You killed Branton!"

I settled my taser on his thigh and gave it a little juice. The jolt was instantaneous. It was enough to shut him up, and he knew it. Once he recovered, and his muscles stopped twitching, he gave me a look that rivaled how a murderer might look at his prey just before he carved them up. "Listen," I said as my skin crawled, "I know you cherish the role of tough guy." *Violent psychopath.* "And I'm sure you knock your family around"—I nodded toward the tin can he called home—"which I'm not a fan of, by the way." My jaw became more set as I continued. "But nobody survives a laser blast to the temple, and I'm ready to give you one." To exaggerate my point, I flicked the safety on and off, so it made a loud clicking sound right next to his ear. "And you already know your brother over there has no issue killing off family members." I ignored Case's indignant huff. "We just need some information, and you're the guy who's going to give it to us. Tandor, a zealot spouting his twisted teachings, was here a few months ago. Some of your family members went with him. We want to know where he came from. There had to be talk after he left."

"I'm not giving you *shit,*" Freedom spat, spittle flying every which way. I brought a forearm up to wipe off my cheek. Without giving him any warning, I plowed my left fist into his jaw, my hand still wrapped around my taser.

When his head stopped moving, blood trickling from a loose tooth or a gash inside his mouth, I said, "Let's try this again. Where did Tandor come from? This is a life-or-death question-and-answer situation. You being the one in danger of dying."

"He's not going to answer," Case growled. "Just to spite me."

"That's right, motherfu—"

I tased Freedom in the leg with a bunch of juice. His body vibrated for four seconds straight before he went limp. He'd be out for another minute or two. I sighed as I stood to address Case. "Having you here is working pretty much the way I thought it would. That craft landed a minute ago. It's not going to take them long to comb this area. Once your totally sweet and not-at-all-insane brother wakes, he's going to be shouting from the hilltops that people who don't belong here are harassing him, and since he can ID you, that's going to be a problem. There's no way the militia will back down in its pursuit of us now."

A small sound came from behind us. A twig breaking.

I spun around, Gem raised.

My gun barrel was aimed at the chest of the woman I'd given the knife to, a boy who looked about four trailing behind her, gripping her skirts. He had blood running down the side of his face. Sampson. "I can help you," she said softly, averting her eyes from my outstretched arm.

I lowered my weapon immediately, feeling sheepish having pointed it at her in the first place. I took a few steps forward. I didn't want to startle her. "Did you hear the question I asked your husband?"

She nodded. "I will tell you, but you must leave quickly once I do. The militia has come to check on us, and nothing must seem amiss, or they will be angry." She turned to Case and surprised me by inclining half her body in a slight bow. "I was never able to thank you for avenging Frankie. What you did was just and good. Did you make Carmen pay for her crime as well?"

He inclined his head right back at her. It must be a Sun Optimist thing. "I did."

"Good." She turned back to me. "Tandor came from a place called Florida. That's the old name for it. We call it Bogland now. There's nothing but water down there. When the seas rose, it covered almost the entire expanse of the peninsula. Only the northern portion is still viable. It's not too far from here. If you follow the coast two hours by craft, you will find it. There's a small tribe living there. The militia that has become our new rulers haven't extended that far. Yet. But they are aggressively trying. Be aware, that tribe has their own protections in place."

"New rulers?" I asked. She'd just confirmed what we'd been thinking. "So, this militia presence is a recent thing?"

"Yes, they came within days of Tandor and the others' departure."

"Do you know what protections this tribe has in place?" Case asked.

Sounds erupted nearby. Possibly a crowd gathering. Shouting followed. "We've heard they favor sonic blasters and bombs. Big ones. Now you must go." She lifted her arms to shoo us backward.

I glanced at Freedom, who was still out cold.

Once he came to, he was going to alert everyone in the vicinity that we'd been here. "What do you want us to do with him?" I asked this nice, helpful woman.

Her face hardened. "I'll take care of him."

"Are you sure?" My voice reflected my intent. I'd do whatever she wanted me to do. Daze came to stand beside us, having completed his gun-disposal task. Sampson ducked around his mother's skirts once he saw Daze and cracked a tentative smile.

"My husband will be out for the rest of the day," she replied confidently. "When he wakes, we will convince him that it was all a dream."

From what I'd just witnessed, Freedom didn't handle many situations with less than full-on rage. Her face changed almost imperceptibly, but I recognized it. In that moment, I knew that even though Freedom was physically stronger, she had the upper hand. I bowed my head, because that's what they did here. "If you need something in the future," I told her, "my name is Holly Danger. If you can get a message to me in the city, I'll help."

"That won't be necessary." She was firm. "When we reach the point of no return, I'll know it."

"And the militia?" I asked.

"We have plans in place to fight back," she said. "We will do what it takes to defend our land and our way of life."

More shouts, closer. It was time to move. I glanced at Case, then back at her. Case apparently didn't have anything to add. "Okay," I conceded. "If we can, we'll try and check back here in a few months." I bent down and smiled at the toddler. "I'll come back and talk to you through the seam in the wall. Does that sound okay? That way, I won't bother your daddy."

The child seemed dismayed that I was addressing him directly. He nodded vigorously, in the way only a small child could, with his entire head, blood-smeared cheek and all. "Bring him back." He pointed at Daze and giggled. "He's my friend."

From Daze's pocket, Maisie said, "I detect fifteen humans within three meters, thirteen humans within twenty meters, and a craft within one kilometer with three occupants on board."

That was our cue to get out. I ignored Sampson's look of sheer confusion at the sound of the automated female voice. I settled my hand on Daze's shoulder. "I hope we can come back someday. Now it's time for us to go." The woman had already started to head back inside, pulling the child along behind her.

I hadn't even gotten her name. Next time. I hurried over to Freedom and jammed my taser into his thigh, giving him one more big dose. Why not help the family out? Then I undid my special rope as quickly as I could and stuffed it back in my pocket.

Case had his Pulse out and was positioned at the corner of the house, head angled to look down the road. "We need to move now." His voice was harsh. Likely, memories of his past dealing with the militia were at the forefront.

"We're right behind you." I ushered Daze in front of me, and we all began to jog. We were lucky the militia had come in at the opposite end of town. They hadn't seen Seven, or they would've gone to investigate, rather than land in town. It seemed Hidden Cove had been a good choice.

I hoped our luck held out.

We traversed the first two kilometers in silence, all of us keeping low, moving quickly, and staying alert. After a particularly sandy and hard-to-traverse hill, we finally stopped to take a short break. "If the rest of your siblings are like Freedom," I said, bending over to brace my hands on my thighs as Daze dropped to the ground wheezing, "then I apologize for thinking that you killed indiscriminately. That guy is insane." I stood and exhaled a few times. I was winded, but not fatigued. You had to be in shape to survive in this world. "And that couldn't have just been from debris denting his head. The eyes say a lot, and his oscillated from vacant to hard-edged and back again in less than a second. If he could've gotten free, he would've inflicted the most pain possible without breaking a sweat."

Case replied, "People lose their humanity out here a hell of a lot quicker than they do in the city."

"My point exactly," I said. "What was Freedom's wife's name, the one I was talking to?"

"Helena—"

Maisie interrupted from Daze's pocket. "UAC with laser capacities detected, closing in quickly. Recommend evacuation immediately. Familiar craft in eight hundred meters. Six minutes until engagement."

UAC with a laser was critically bad news. I had one of those, and it was deadly.

Case took off, shouting, "I'll have her up and ready in five."

I hauled Daze off the ground, pulling him behind me as we raced forward, my hand clasped around his. "Come on, kid, you can do it. When we get back to the city, I'm going to have you run circuits. Being in shape will save your scrawny hide. It's one of the main reasons I'm still alive."

"I…can do it," he huffed, managing to keep up.

"I know…you can," I replied between gasps. "But just to be sure…I'm not letting go."

We were ten meters shy of Seven when I finally heard the props. The distinct thrumming was loud, indicating the size of the UAC.

I shoved Daze in front of me. "Get in!" Once he cleared the door, I dove into the passenger seat.

Right as a laser blast struck the ground where my feet had been.

Chapter 11

Case had us airborne within ten seconds. There'd been no time to strap in as he jammed the levers, turning sharply to avoid laser fire. I tumbled into his lap. "Great," I muttered, clawing my way back to my own seat.

"Hold on," he ground out as he shot us straight up. Then he leveled out and hit the hydro-boost. My head flung back into the headrest as we rocketed away.

I took a moment to gather myself, taking a few deep breaths, trying to steady my heartbeat. I watched as Case inched us closer and closer to the clouds. My head whipped around. "You're not going back in the clouds again, are you? We're going too fast."

"It's the only way to lose our tail completely," he said, his voice tight.

I arched my neck to look out the rear window. I couldn't spot anything behind us, because we were moving too quickly. "You just boosted," I argued.

"There's no way that thing can catch up to us." Below, the landscape was a blur.

"I'm not heading into the clouds to get away from the UAC," he said. "The dronecraft that landed in town will be chasing us as soon as they can."

"I don't think Helena is going to tell them we were there."

"She won't have to," he answered as the front of the craft touched the wispy, white tendrils. "If that UAC shoots lasers that accurately, they have a live video feed. It might be spotty, but they know where we are and will send that craft after us."

I sat back and tried to resign myself to my fate in the clouds. But this time I refused to pass out. "No hyperventilating," I muttered to myself. "You can do this."

"What?" Case asked, distracted.

"Nothing," I said, trying to get my mind on something else—like the future. "Are you familiar with this place Helena was talking about? Florida?"

"A bit," he said as the craft was consumed by white, our visibility down to nothing but a few meters in front of us. Once we were completely ensconced, he hit the radio-frequency button and the dash went dark. "My Sun Optimist family traveled there a couple of times over the years, but we never went into a town. Helena was right, there's nothing but water down there, for the most part. Almost all the land that far south was at sea level. When the oceans rose, it was swallowed up."

Maisie announced from the backseat, "There are no

crafts or UACs in the area. Female, Holly, heart rate eighty-five beats per minute. Blood pressure one hundred sixty-eight systolic, eighty-nine diastolic. Rapid respiration. Hydration recommended."

I turned around in my seat to where Daze held Maisie cradled in his lap. "Why only me? Huh, Maisie? What about the males in the craft? Surely their stats are just as necessary to broadcast. And I can't possibly be the only one who needs to stay hydrated."

She replied, "Child, Daze, and male, Case, heart rates elevated but stable, blood pressure within normal range. Hydration recommended."

"See?" I grumbled, "I'm not the only one who needs water. But how about from now on we keep my stats private unless I ask, okay, Maisie?"

"Noted," Maisie replied. "Holly vitals to be repeated only when necessary."

"No," I objected, trying to regulate my voice so as not to get into an argument with an inanimate object—however brilliant she was. "Holly's vitals will only be announced upon request by Holly herself. That's an order, Maisie. I mean it." Man, this was getting strange. I was ordering her around like a real human being.

"Noted," Maisie said. "Holly vitals repeated only upon request."

Before I could object to the word *repeated* again, Daze interjected, smiling, his voice excited. "See? She's learning. It's not perfect, but I mean, she's over sixty years old. I think it's impressive. She'll get better at following directions. I know she will."

I turned to face the front, crossing my arms. "If she learns to keep my stats to herself, I'll consider it impressive," I replied. Case chuckled, seeming to relax by a few degrees. I tried to follow suit, but the view in front of me, nothing but lightness as far as we could see, which was only a few meters in front of us, was unsettling. I leaned my head against the rest, tilting it toward Case. "Sure, you can laugh now, but wait until she calls you out for no reason."

"She's taken a liking to you," Case said, humor still in his voice. "She's trying to keep you safe. You should probably drink some water."

I snorted. "She's a robot. She shouldn't have favorites. To her, we should all just be humans."

He shrugged. "Maybe because she's been programmed to be female, she has a soft spot for other females. There is a difference, you know."

From the backseat, Maisie spouted, "Females and males are fundamentally different. Females have mammary glands necessary for the production of milk, and sexual organs to facilitate—"

"Stop, Maisie," I commanded, thankful she immediately ceased speaking. "No need for a male-versus-female discussion at the moment. We'll let you know if and when we need to be educated on that front." I needed a topic change, and fast, preferably one that Maisie couldn't participate in. I asked Case, "Do you think Tandor's father is still alive? Or do you think we'll hit a dead end?"

"Hard to know," Case answered as he began our

descent out of the clouds, much to my relief. "Tandor was definitely not all there, but he was educated. I've heard tales over the years about the tribe down there. When I was in my early teens, we heard a rumor that it was made up of scientists and mathematicians on the run from the government. We never encountered them, as I said, but it would make sense, given what Tandor was in possession of. As for his father being alive? I have no idea."

Daze piped in, "My dad was a scientist. At least I think he was. My mom said he was good at math. And he worked for the government for a while." His tone was more than glum. Poor kid. I understood how bad it sucked not to know your dad.

I turned. Daze's father being a scientist was interesting information. "What else do you know about him?" I asked.

"Not much," Daze replied, fiddling with the ends of the cloth separating his body from Maisie—who was thankfully quiet. "My mom never wanted to talk about it. The only information I ever got was when she was talking to somebody else and she didn't think I was listening." He sounded a little defeated. I'm sure he regretted not pressing his mother more before she died. "She was mad at him for leaving."

"Did she think the government did something to him?" I asked. That happened often enough. "Or did he go on his own?"

Daze shrugged. "I don't know. But he left one day and never came back."

My eyebrows rose. I didn't want to upset the kid by informing him a scientist would have likely taken his supercomputer with him if he'd gone on the run. My guess was the government had interfered. Maybe Daze's dad had uncovered some corruption or found out something he shouldn't have. It was impossible to know. Gently, I asked, "Why do you think he left his pico behind?"

Daze picked up a cup and turned it over in his hands. "I think, maybe…he wanted to give me and my mom a chance."

"I'm sure he did," I said. "I'll tell you what, when we get back to the city, I'll look into it. You met Claire already. I bet she can help us figure out which department your dad worked for. You said you were named Robert, after your dad. Do you remember your surname?"

Before Daze could answer, and just as Case cleared the clouds fully, Maisie erupted, "The barometer is dropping, precipitation is imminent. The temperature is fifteen degrees Celsius."

"Any crafts in the area?" Case asked.

Maisie replied, "I detect no crafts in the area."

Case turned the power back on, and everything sprang to life. The readout on the dash said that we were heading straight east.

"Are you heading to the sea?" I asked.

"Yes," Case answered. "That's the easiest way. If there's a tribe down there, they're likely going to be located close to the ocean. If Tandor's father was working on a cure for Plush, based on the formula we saw, and sodium alginate was necessary, it would be located by saltwater."

I turned to the kid once again. "While you were being held against your will, did Tandor ever mention his dad? Did you overhear anything?"

He shook his head. "No. Tandor acted like he was a god. I didn't even know he had a dad." The kid looked thoughtful. "But one time he did say something about the 'hovel' he was forced to grow up in. He sounded angry about it, but I didn't know what a hovel was. I'd never heard that word before."

Before I could elaborate, Maisie said, "A hovel is a simply constructed dwelling, often small, squalid, and unpleasant. Can be humble, dirty, and disorganized. Not recommended as a residence."

"There you have it," I said, chuckling. It was nice to have a dictionary handy. "So he mentioned living in a hovel? Anything else?"

"He kind of made it sound like it was underground."

"Keep talking."

"I don't remember much else," Daze said. "I wish I did. He just said he was done living in a hovel and he'd be damned if he had to live underground like a hibernating rat again."

"Rats do not hibernate," Maisie explained. "Hibernating animals include bears—"

"Stop, Maisie," I said. She complied, and just to ensure a little Maisie-free time, I ordered in an unnecessarily firm tone, "You will remain quiet for the next ten minutes, unless an emergency arises. If a craft or a UAC enters the area, you can alert us. Otherwise, remain silent." Her lights dimmed, and I shrugged, not knowing if the request would take or not, but glad I'd tried. I focused my attention back on Daze. "Keep thinking about it. Maybe something will come to you."

"Okay, I will," he said.

I glanced out the window. In the distance, the ocean consumed all the available horizon. The sea was dark green, almost black. The waves were roiling, whitecaps crashing down everywhere my eyes tracked. Before I'd met Case, I'd been to the ocean only one other time, when I was young. Bender had taken me there to see its wrath. It had been a terrifying sight. But this time, I felt more in control of myself. "It seems my body is trying to make peace with the ocean," I mumbled.

"Maisie could prove that," Case joked. "All we have to do is ask her."

"Very funny," I said. "But it's true. It still scares me, but I'm less worried."

"If it makes you feel any better, I plan on hugging the coast, not going over open water," Case said. "There are no crafts around, and we need to be on the lookout for any human structures. We can't see those if we're over the sea."

Even better.

"Anything is fine with me." I shrugged. "I mean it. Pulse rate is steady."

Case gave a full-throated laugh. "We'll see about that."

Chapter 12

My brain worked overtime trying to figure out how we were going to achieve our goals, so when the craft dropped altitude abruptly, I was startled. We'd been flying for almost two hours. I glanced over at Case. I couldn't see his eyes, so I didn't know if he was fatigued, but he seemed to be in control.

I leaned forward in my seat, glancing at the dash, combing the ground below for any signs of life, like I'd been doing for hours, seeing only sand and sea. "Helena said that this tribe favors sonic blasters and bombs," I said. "Do you think they have rocket launchers? Or will they only be an issue on land?"

"I'm sure they have launchers," he said, his voice raspy from not speaking much over the last hour. "My plan is to stick to the sand. As we get closer, we should see signs of human habitation. Flying directly over the town wouldn't be advisable, but might not be avoidable. I'll land at the first signs of life, preferably beforehand."

"Does anything look familiar?" I asked. "I mean, since you were here all those years ago?"

"Not yet, but if memory serves," he answered, "there will be several large sand dunes, along with the wreckage of what might've been some sort of resort."

I scanned below as far as I could see, targeting my eyes in a grid, like I'd been trained to do. We were looking for any hints that humans were currently living down there. If people were around, the topography should go from random to organized. That's what people did, even when they weren't trying to—they organized their space.

We flew for a while in silence, my eyes working overtime. I knew Case was doing the same. Daze scooted to the side right behind me and peered out the passenger window.

After what seemed like an hour, but was likely only twenty minutes, I spotted something. "There," I said, jabbing my finger ahead of us. "I think I see something. It doesn't look like more than a few lumps, but that area definitely looks different than everything around it. It almost looks like a dome. It might be nothing, but we should check."

Case immediately took us down, slowing our speed as he flew us over half sand and half-dead vegetation. The beach was wide, the sea crashing three hundred meters to our left as we neared the definite manmade objects.

"What's the plan?" I asked. "Are we going to land?"

Case eased Seven straight down. "Yes. We should

check it out. But we have to be on high alert. We don't know how much firepower they have." The craft made a soft landing on the spongy ground. The landscape was nothing but gently rolling dunes dotted with scrubby, dead bushes. We were approximately a half kilometer away from the strange domes. I could see the tops of two, which were partially hidden by the short rises. "On foot will be the safest."

"Agreed," I said, lofting my door. "Those domes could very well be empty, but my guess is there's something beneath them worth investigating. We've been in the craft for the right amount of time. We should be in the vicinity of the tribe, depending on how close they are to the sea."

We all piled out.

I stretched my cramped legs. I'd never sat for this long in a craft before. In the city, I was always on the move. Without glancing behind me, where I knew Daze was, I asked, "Maisie, do you detect any human signatures? Feel free to skip the three of us."

Daze came up beside me as Maisie replied, "I detect three humans within three meters and one human within one hundred meters."

My eyebrows shot upward. There was someone here, but an individual only, rather than a tribe.

"What do you think that means? Only one person," I said to Case, who was busy covering Seven with the reflective cloth he'd brought with us. It was windy here, and he was doing his best to secure it with small clamps he'd had in the back.

"I don't know," he answered. "People need tribes to survive. Life is too brutal to live out here alone. So, even though the status reader's only picking up one signature now, it could be that the rest of the tribe is just out of her reach, or they're out on a mission."

Once he was done, we began to move.

I withdrew my Gem. We had no idea what we were in for, and it was better to be prepared. "Maisie, which direction is the human within one hundred meters?"

"South by southwest," she answered.

The dead scrub popped and crackled underneath our boots as we walked. It was slow-going, the roots intermixed with sand making the ground bumpy and brittle, like a burn that'd never healed. "I wonder why someone would choose to live so close to the sea. If there was another cataclysmic event, certainly a tsunami could reach those domes."

"People are creatures of habit," Case replied, shrugging. "They stick to what they know, and these were likely built long ago. Change is hard."

"Even though humans are resistant to change"—which I knew to be true based on my own experiences—"our survival instinct overrides everything else—or it should."

"You're right," he said. "We won't know until we get there and find out." Case had his Pulse out, too. Neither of us were willing to take any chances.

We trudged over a particularly large patch of black, crunchy, strawlike grass as the sea crashed behind us at regular intervals, shooting its dense, salty air up our nostrils. "If Tandor was raised here, in order to get up north to your old tribe and then on to the city, he had to have access to multiple crafts. So maybe the tribe is spread out."

"That's my guess," Case conceded. "We're going to have to be extremely careful moving forward. If luck is on our side, we landed at the very edge of habitation in these parts."

We crested a short hill, and the tops of the domes we'd seen from the sky came crisply into view. They were perfect ovals. They weren't very tall, no more than three meters at the crest.

One was positioned closer to the sea, the other directly behind it.

As we approached, we could see they'd been meticulously smoothed over and cared for. With the weather being what it was, keeping something like that looking good would take maintenance.

"Maisie, how close is the human signature now?" I asked my new best friend.

"I detect three humans within three meters." Okay, not *best*. She had a ways to go to earn that title. "I detect one human within ten meters."

"Is the human underground?" Case asked, his tone quiet, his Pulse aimed forward. His steps were cautious, as were mine.

I glanced behind me when the status reader didn't respond. The kid held Maisie out in his hand. I repeated Case's question.

Within moments, Maisie lit up and replied, "The

human I detect has a barrier made of carbon, earth, and human matter."

I wasn't sure I wanted to know what the human matter was. I snickered at Case. "I don't think Maisie likes you. She totally ignored your question." He probably hadn't spoken loud enough for her to hear. I addressed Daze. "You need to take cover while we approach whoever this is. If something happens, get back to the craft. I haven't given you flying lessons yet, but I know you can figure it out. Are we clear?" He had Maisie, after all.

"Clear." His voice was thin, but confident. When we got home, after laser-gun training, I was going to teach the kid how to pilot a craft. I'd learned at age ten. Piloting was tricky at first, but once you learned the basics, it all came together. It was something he'd have to know. It could be the difference between living and dying.

Flying out of a bad situation was often the best chance of survival.

Daze made his way toward a small hill that he could crouch behind. I was impressed with the fact that he understood that these kinds of situations called for caution and that if we were trying to protect him, we'd have a hard time protecting ourselves.

As Case and I crept closer, he went left, while I circled right.

We headed toward the dome that was farther inland. That would be about ten meters, according to what Maisie had told us. We met up around the front, where a single titanium door was set into the structure, smartly facing away from the sea.

Maybe they did have precautions in place in case of another surge. Now that I could accurately see the distance, the sea was fairly far away, and the domes were up a small incline.

The door was set at an angle, following the curve of the dome. It looked a little surreal. There were no windows or any remnants of anything artificial or human-made lying around, just earth and scrub.

"Well, are we just going to knock?" I asked. "I have a feeling that door has got a thick layer of graphene behind it. I'm sure whoever is inside has protected themselves." It was a little odd to stand out here exposed, but what else were we going to do? If a bomb went off, it would become a very bad day.

Instead of answering, Case moved forward, settling his hand on the lever. It was a crazy move, because it could be rigged. I felt like telling him that, but I kept my mouth shut.

Nothing happened. He rattled it, but it was locked. He turned to me. "I'll knock while you circle around back. There's no reason both of us should be in the line of fire."

"It doesn't matter if I'm around back or not. We could both be blown to hell in seconds," I countered. "I'll stay. You knock, and I'll aim my gun. If anybody comes through that door with harmful intent, they'll be down before they know what happened." I scanned the dome again. "I don't see any tech." There were no radio antennas, cameras, or monitors attached to the walls. "Whoever exists here lives a crude existence."

Case nodded, then took the butt of his Pulse and rammed it against the metal door a few times. Hollow sounds echoed out. Whoever was down there had to have heard that. He took a step back, his arms out in front of him, barrel aimed. His gun was disgusting. It liquefied your insides. Totally effective, but a horrible way to go.

We waited for what seemed like an hour, but in reality, only two minutes passed. I was just about to nod to Case to try again when a loud *thunk* sounded from somewhere inside. A lock being retracted. The door began to swing outward.

I stopped breathing for a second.

Being here wasn't anything like in the city, where there were places to hide and protect yourself. We were standing out in the open. Anything could happen. I was glad the kid wasn't around.

A shock of white hair was the first indication that someone was coming through the door. "No need to aim your guns at me. I'm unarmed." His voice sounded weary and frail, a grizzled hand curling around the doorframe as he took his time guiding it open.

Once I glimpsed his face, I started breathing again, my mouth tumbling open.

If I'd thought Cozzi was old, this guy was ancient. He had to be at least twenty years older. I'd never seen anyone reach that age before. Life-spans in the city were much shorter. People just didn't live to see their doddering years. Unlike our ancestors, who'd lived well into their hundreds. When you could print new organs, longevity took on new meaning.

He finally stepped over the threshold and drew himself up, looking us straight in the eyes. But he wasn't able to get fully erect. His back was hunched, a padded mass visible over his left shoulder. His clothing hung off of his thin frame, several sizes too big. It didn't look like this environment had done him any favors, although he was still alive, so that was something. "I said there's no need to aim your weapons at me," he wheezed, taking another shuffling step forward.

My gaze slipped to Case as I lowered my Gem. Case's arms went down as well. Even if this guy decided to pull a weapon on us, we'd see him telegraph it with enough time to retaliate.

"Are you alone here, old man?" Case asked with genuine curiosity.

"Yes. This is my home," he said quietly. I had to strain to hear him.

"Your tribe can't be too far away," I countered. "You can't live out here alone."

"I'm not part of any tribe," he snarled, getting feisty, which was better since I could hear him more clearly when he was angry. "I've been living in here, in this dome, on my own for the last forty-three years."

My face reflected my surprise. I took a few steps forward. "How do you get enough food and water out here by yourself?"

"I have everything I need below," he replied. "I get along just fine."

"Nobody comes to check on you?" Case asked, his voice full of the same skepticism.

"Occasionally, a soul will drift by," he conceded. "But not too often."

"So, you're admitting that there's a tribe nearby," I said. A soul didn't just *drift* by in a remote place like this. There was definitely more to the story, but he didn't trust us yet. I didn't blame him. The more I studied him, the more ancient and grizzled he seemed. His hair stuck up in tufts all over his head. Skin sagged around his face, and his eyes were heavily lidded and creased from the passing of time. He was surviving, but it didn't exactly look like a stellar life.

I whistled, alerting Daze that the coast was clear.

"Yes," the man answered cagily. "There are people nearby."

He was playing with us. "We just came to ask you a few questions. We mean no harm," I said. "We know there's a tribe near here, which you've now confirmed, possibly made up of scientists a long time ago." I didn't add that he looked like he fit the description of a scientist, especially if one inserted the word *mad* in front of it. "We need to know if there's one who had a child by the name of Tandor. It could be a surname, we're not sure. It's critical we find his father, or his old residence, and time is of the essence."

The old man squinted at me, his eyelids almost fully covering his eyes, like I was trying to deceive him. He studied me, analyzing if what I was saying was true or not. His expression took on a hardened look, which was impressive since his skin was so slack.

I could see the moment he decided he wasn't going to cooperate.

His bushy white eyebrows shot up while his lips went down, forming a nice, tight line. He didn't have any allegiance to us. He owed us nothing.

At that moment, Daze barreled around the corner, out of breath and grinning. "I just saw the coolest thing!" he called as he ran, oblivious to anything around him. We were going to have to work on that. Just because I'd whistled didn't mean he could launch himself freely into the fray without checking it out first. "I was watching the sea, and it lit up. I swear! There were all these small dots, and they blinked yellow. I saw it! I'm not lying." He skidded to a stop in front of us.

I watched the old man's face as he took in the child. It changed almost imperceptibly, but it was enough.

We had an in.

Daze was the piece we needed to get through the door.

I ruffled the kid's hair, redirecting him around so he was positioned in front of the stranger. "I believe you. Blinking yellow in the sea is a good thing," I told him. "This is…" I inclined my head toward the man.

"Walt," the old man answered.

"Walt was just about to invite us inside."

Chapter 13

When Walt didn't graciously offer to usher us into his dome home, I settled both my hands on Daze's shoulders and propelled him forward. "Daze, go show Walt what Maisie can do." Getting this stubborn old man to cooperate with us was going to take some finesse.

"Um, okay." Without hesitation, the kid fished the status egg out of his pocket as he moved. Daze wasn't even tentative about it. He darted up to the man like they'd been friends forever. I smiled.

As Daze unwrapped the prize, Case moved to stand next to me. "What are you doing?" he asked, his voice low. "We don't need to get inside. We just need him to answer a few questions, then we can move on."

"I'm building trust. You should take notes," I whispered. "This guy knows the answers to our questions. I can see it in his eyes. But he's not ready to help us. He's been around a long time, and I want more than a few questions answered. I want a conversation. He could be Tandor's father, for all we know. He's certainly old enough. Five minutes with Daze and we're in, I guarantee it." I shot Case a questioning glance. "Aren't you at all curious about what he has down there?" I motioned toward the dome. "I mean, how has he survived out here for all these years on his own? Yeah, he doesn't look like he's in the greatest shape, but look how old he is. People in the city don't live that long." So many questions. "You said there was a rumor about scientists living here. When I just mentioned it, he wasn't surprised at all. His bushy eyebrows didn't even waggle. We just need to gain a little trust, then the answers will be ours."

Daze was busy chattering, his palms lofted forward. Walt bent over, reaching his hand out. "You can't touch it," Daze cautioned. "The oil on your fingertips can mess up the sensors."

"No, they won't, boy," Walt said, plucking the egg up in his fist. "These things were made with silica-shell technology. It's durable, like triple-extra-hard polymer, and allows the owner to interact however they wish, protecting everything inside."

I elbowed Case and inclined my head. "See? He knows stuff. My money is on him being a scientist."

"Fine," Case said. "But we can't stay out here all day. If anyone comes to investigate, it's going to be an issue."

I turned in a circle, shielding my eyes with my hand to keep some of the precip off my face, since I had my visor retracted. "It looks like there's a path in the scrub over there." I gestured to the side, trying to be discreet. "If people stop by once in a while, they must come that way. It must be close enough to walk."

"Could be, or they could have a craft," Case said.

"Walt's going to help us," I said. "I'm sure of it. But maybe we can offer him something to close the deal. You have some spare clothes in the craft. How about we offer him new duds in exchange for the information we need?"

Case made a face. "I'm not giving that old man my clothing," he said. "Not to mention, everything I have would droop more on him than what he's already wearing."

That was true.

Case was a big man, and Walt was little more than a stooped-over skeleton. I shrugged. "Well, I'm sure there's something we can find that he'd be willing to trade for. People always need something. And being so far out, there is a high likelihood we have something he'll bargain for."

Daze's voice went up several octaves. "Holly! You have to see this." I placed my Gem in my waistband and made my way to his side. "Do it again, Walt," the kid commanded.

Walt held Maisie in his hand. "Status reader, access your archives." The egg lit up, shooting colors every which way. "Give us the sound of a horse."

A moment later, there was a distinct whinny.

I knew it was the right noise, because I'd heard

horses sound exactly like that in the video feed I played on my wall screen at my residence in the canals.

Daze glanced at me, his eyes wide. "She has tons of memory. Way more than we thought."

"This is a special egg. It's a military special. You can see by these markings right here." Walt turned the egg over and pointed to some micro-etchings that consisted of barely legible letters and numerals.

"You've had some experience with status readers," I said to Walt.

"Sure," he replied casually, his voice full of the kind of vibration that comes with old age, each syllable shaking slightly. "I even helped design some. Once upon a time, my brain was pretty quick. Not so much anymore." He scratched his head, causing his sparse hair to spread in different directions.

"You're a scientist, then?" I asked carefully. I didn't want to spook him when it seemed he was warming to us.

"I guess that's a fair assessment," he replied as he turned toward the opening of his home. "A bit more than that, some would say. I was an astrophysicist in my former life. Ironically, I studied the stars and their trajectory in my early years, but I couldn't stop the meteor from decimating this planet." There was a real sadness in his voice. "I don't call myself an astrophysicist anymore. When you can't see the sky, there's nothing much to study. I'm simply a scientist."

"How old are you?" I asked.

The old man took a step over the threshold. "I lost

track of birthdays long ago. But I'm pushing the century mark, as far as I can gather." He arced a gnarled hand in front of him as he began to descend. "What are you waiting for? Come in and get out of the rain. Close up behind you."

Daze followed along happily, a constant stream of chatter ensuing.

I went next, giving Case a casual *I told you so* nod as he followed.

The steps were utilitarian, metal with a sharp descent, handrails on both sides. Case shut the door with a loud clank, engaging the giant dead bolt behind him.

Once we were at the bottom, the space opened up far beyond the confines of the dome above, much larger than I'd anticipated. It was brightly lit. In fact, there were lights all over. Some regular, some UV. I knew they were UV because of the pale-yellow glow they emitted. But also, because they were illuminating plants.

Green plants.

Real vegetation.

I rushed over to one of the long tables that held several large lamps, trying to regain the breath that had just left my body. "You're growing things down here?" I exclaimed.

"Of course I am," he replied, shuffling to my side. "The whole world should be growing things."

I turned, sputtering, "But…but…there's not enough UV bulbs to go around. And no seeds." I shouldn't have to state the obvious to a scientist.

Although, it was rumored that the government had access to seeds, but what they did with them was a mystery.

"Yes," he agreed. "It's a terrible thing that we don't have enough light. No one anticipated a disaster such as this, so the quantities of UV lamps were not nearly on the scale we needed. It's a real problem." The old man's tone turned jovial, surprising me. "But with the light we do have, we should be constantly growing things!" He held up a single gnarled finger to emphasize his point. "That's the problem with the world today. We don't look to the future. We only focus on the here and now. The seeds we do have will multiply if they are allowed to grow. The problem solves itself." Walt walked over to another table that held a bunch of seedlings, lightly pressing the soft growth between his fingertips and sighing.

I turned around, gripping the table for support, as I took in the rest of the room. It was a full-blown laboratory, at least five times bigger than the dome above us, spreading out under the earth.

It was divided into stations, each one dedicated to something unique.

Walt was a busy man, and I was in awe.

Case moved to another table, his face full of the kind of wonder that had to mirror my own. "You're making slurry?" he asked, stopping at a table that held a large 3-D bio-printer. Case picked up something. It looked amazing—like *real* food.

Not a protein cake.

Food *food*.

It was a rich black color, not the molten brown we were used to.

I rushed toward him, almost without knowing I was moving. "What is that?" I said, my voice low, like if I said anything too loudly, the thing in his hand would disappear.

Walt chuckled as he made his way toward us. "Go ahead, take a bite."

Case glanced at it skeptically, bringing it to his nose to take a sniff. Then he broke the thing in half. It came apart freely, not crumbling at all, and he handed a piece to me. The inside looked soft and spongy. It was black and shaped like a ball but with a square bottom.

I held it to my nose, like Case had.

It smelled good, but I didn't have a name for it. I'd never scented anything like it before. I further broke my piece in half and handed a portion to Daze, who'd come to stand by us.

Tentatively, I put it to my lips.

Once inside my mouth, it disintegrated over my tongue, the flavor sweet and delicious. I closed my eyes, and a low hum issued from my throat. I savored the texture, wanting to remember how it tasted. I barely had to chew. It was over too soon. I opened my eyes. "What *was* that?"

Walt appeared delighted. "That, my girl, was a chocolate cupcake. Back in my day, we had an abundance of them at places called bakeries. They produced sweet confections like that on a daily basis, in mass quantities. With the invention of bio-printers, anything was possible, and even the lowliest baker could become a master."

"I don't understand," I said as Daze made a sound of delight next to me. "How do you have the ability to make food taste delicious? All the city can make are dry, crumbly protein cakes."

"Like your husband said"—Walt gestured at Case—"it's about the slurry. These old printers were finicky." He affectionately patted the machine on the table. "Most of them were in desperate need of upgrades before that fateful day. They required that the molecules come separated before you added them to the printer. If you didn't separate, it couldn't make heads or tails of what you wanted, so it just blurred everything together. It made food—just not food that tasted very good. The protein cakes of today." He slid the empty plate to the side. "In the days leading up to the meteor strike, the slurry came individually packaged. It was produced in specialized facilities and shipped out the moment you needed it. Then, according to a particular recipe, you added the exact portions of the right things. We don't have that luxury today, and no one remembers or has the means to separate the atoms on a molecular scale."

I glanced at the empty plate, longing for more of that unbelievable cupcake. "How do you separate them?"

"I have a micro-centrifuge—but more importantly, I know the recipes. All the information is right where I need it." He tapped a bent finger against his temple. "It's been some of my life's work to perfect the bioprinting process. I think I've done a magnificent job. I watched you enjoy that cupcake, and that makes me proud."

"I did enjoy it. Congratulations," I said. "Your life's work is delicious." Nutrients coupled with flavor was an entirely new concept. "Can I ask how you ended up here?" I glanced around the room again.

His face grew serious as he shuffled over to a chair, turning to sit slowly. "I left the city during a very dark time—fled is more accurate. Immediately following the disaster, there was widespread panic and desperation, as you can imagine. But once that subsided, a sense of communal purpose grew. We all banded together with the sole endeavor of saving the human race." He shook his head sadly. "But it didn't last for more than three to four years at most. As the resources dwindled, different factions vied for power. There was warring within the government. Darkness and greed took over, and we scientists escaped before we were killed, or worse. The folks who had gained control weren't interested in science or furthering mankind. They believed the world would come to an end sooner than later, so why bother? They craved power, hoarding what resources they could. Any who opposed would be killed. It's not like we were living quiet lives. We were working for the government. We were forced to make a choice. Coming here meant we could carry on our work."

"How many years ago was that?" Case asked. "I can understand escaping when times are tough, but once the government changed over and again established aid for the people, why didn't you return?"

"Well, by that time, we'd established ourselves here." He shrugged his thin shoulders. "Many years went into building these dome homes. We had a small but viable community. We were busy working on cures, food solutions, AI and LiveBot-compatible software, everything you can dream of. We were doing our best to find a way to move this decimated planet forward and felt that doing it from here was just as effective. Who knew when the government would change once again?"

"We appreciate your efforts to continue your work against all odds," I said. "But how were you planning on sharing everything you've learned with the rest of the population? The city, which has nearly forty thousand residents, less than in your time I'm sure, sinks deeper into ruins with each passing year. We're facing full extinction in a very short period of time." I walked over to a chair opposite Walt's and sat, sliding off my helmet. "No one has benefited from your efforts, at least that I've seen. Why is that?"

He scratched his head. "That's not an easy question to answer. The years went by very quickly, it's true. We were making real progress, and then...Goldbright happened."

"Goldbright?" I prodded when he didn't readily proceed.

"He led us astray, you see," Walt said.

I didn't see, but I gave him time to answer.

"We gave him our data, our experiments, our *seeds*." Walt gestured to the station set up with the ultraviolet lights, emerald-green tendrils brimming out of carbon pots. I'd honestly never seen anything so invigoratingly beautiful. It was the same color green as the grass in the video feed on my screen at home, and I was having a hard time believing it actually existed in our world today. "He said he was taking our findings to the city, sharing them with the government and with other scientists who remained there. He came back many times to report that our work was helping people in need, and like fools, we believed him." Walt appeared defeated, his shoulders drooping even more.

"What happened then?" Case asked gently, leaning back against the edge of the stairwell, crossing his arms. We were all rapt. It seemed this man had lived through it all.

"He left." Walt's voice was nothing more than a shaky whisper.

"Left where?" I asked.

But I already knew.

"The Flotilla." The old man slumped forward, the lump on his back looking cumbersome. He looked like he'd topple off that chair if he so much as sneezed. "Goldbright took years upon years of our work and sailed away without looking back." Sounded like a familiar story. "We were devastated."

The Water Initiative, in which the wealthy had

taken all the boats, along with all the resources they could gather—including all valuable medical supplies, engineering tools, inoculations, scientific research—and floated them out to sea, was continuing to ruin lives thirty years after it had set sail.

Water communities hadn't been a foreign concept in our ancestors' world. Before the dark days, people had been cultivating life on the ocean for years. As far as history stated, those communities had flourished. The individuals, referred to as sea farmers or hydro-farmers, had successfully farmed vegetables and the high-nutrient seaweed we were here to find.

I'd once seen a picture of a floating home. It'd been spherical, the living space completely clear, set half above, half below the waterline, with a large circular deck that kept it afloat. It'd had solar panels on the roof and water-purification systems built in. It had looked peaceful and serene.

No remnants of these places or homes had survived the meteor and its aftereffects.

I rested my back against the chair. "Why didn't you go with them?" I asked. There was no doubt he'd been asked. They would've wanted any and all scientists to join them, without exception.

"Because my place was here," he stated firmly. "With the people."

"But there's no people here," Daze said, speaking for the first time, gazing around the space as if to make sure we simply hadn't noticed more individuals in here with us.

"Yes, well." Walt bobbed his head, his wispy white hair defying gravity as it wafted around his head. "The days and months got away from us. After Goldbright left, we had no more communication with the city, no crafts to speak of. We had no idea what happened when the Flotilla left. I envisioned a total collapse of the city. Then, ten years ago, a full twenty years after The Water Initiative left, a new scientist joined our ranks, filling us in with stories of another corrupt government—the one he was running from. A few years after that, we were taken over by a small militia. Then my friend Ronston, a fellow scientist, died." He gestured casually to the right, which I assumed indicated the other dome, and bowed his head in defeat. "It was easier to continue working here, and in the end, after so many years, I have to admit I was a coward. Too frightened and too old to deal with what I assumed to be chaos in the city. You have a right to call me out. I've failed the human race, which is just irony, when it has always been my agenda to save it."

I stood. "You're no coward, and you haven't failed anyone," I told him firmly. "What you've been able to achieve here is nothing short of miraculous. And who knows? Maybe if you had gone to the city earlier, your research would've stopped or you would've been killed. There's no way to know for sure. But we've found you now, and if it's still your wish, we will see to it that you and your research get safely to the city, where you can be of the most help to others. You have my word and my protection."

He slowly lifted his head, nodding, hair waving. "I would like that," he said. "To see the city again before I die is my greatest wish."

"Then we'll make it happen," I said. "But there's one thing we need clarification on right away. The militia you mentioned. We need to know everything about it and the remaining tribe members and any other scientists who live here." I began to pace. "We came here hoping you could tell us about a person named Tandor. We think his father might've been a scientist." I turned to meet Walt's startled gaze. There was some recognition there, and that gave me hope we were on the right track. "We're here to find sodium alginate, but if your tribe has been infiltrated by a militia, our first priority will be to make sure your community is safe."

Chapter 14

Walt stood, making his way to a table that held glass vials filled with colored liquids, and all but growled, "We scientists found this place all those years ago because the good people who lived here originally welcomed us. Without their help, none of this would've been possible." He made a frail, sweeping gesture around his dome. "Some talented engineers helped us make these durable, long-lasting homes that can weather any storm—short of full catastrophe, of course. The community at the time was over a hundred strong, survivors to the bone. They knew how to work." He shook his head wistfully. "Many of the original members have died, as well as many scientists, but the remaining inhabitants, somewhere around twenty, have been infested by a small militia group for going on five or six years now. Horrid people, for the most part. They live for violence and practice oppression with a strong arm. After their infiltration of the tribe, they found out about us scientists—myself, my old friend Ronston"—he gestured to the right again absentmindedly—"and three others, although one fellow died just a few months ago. The newcomer who arrived ten years ago. It was a shame to lose him. He was a brilliant mathematician. So, that makes three of us scientists alive now, including myself. Once upon a time, I believe there were twelve of us." He cleared his throat as he waved a hand. "Anyway, these awful militia men have run us into the ground demanding our services." Walt made his way back to his seat. "But by complying with their orders, we've done nothing but a disservice to ourselves, because now they've gotten used to all of the comforts we bring them. They kill for indiscriminate reasons, with brutal force and violence, and have, from what I've seen, managed to convert many of the remaining tribesmen to their cause. Certainly upon threat at first, but they have cleverly turned this once hardworking tribe into nothing more than a lazy, demanding population. It's nothing like it used to be. I look forward to vacating the area."

"We will get you out, I promise," I told him. "It will take us some time to make sure it's safe in the city, but we will get you out." The story Walt had just recounted was fairly dire, the militia being a big complication. But, as he'd spoken, it had become clear to me that Tandor had indeed originated from here—as possibly one of the tribe's original members, as a child of one of the scientists, like we thought. I turned to Case. "What Walt said makes sense. I'm pretty sure this is why Tandor was so cocky and overly confident when he left this place." I paced as I put my thoughts together. "I bet the militia members who stayed behind were waiting for him to take over the government, so they could come up and bolster his agenda when the coup was over. Then Tandor would be in control of all this." I made a sweeping gesture to encompass Walt's home and the dome next door. "He also knew everything here would be well protected until he needed it." It was a sobering thought. If Tandor had completed his mission successfully and brought these valuable resources to the city, everyone would've been at his mercy. He would've used food, inoculations, and Plush, among other things, as weapons of punishment and to incite loyalty.

The city would've become a war zone.

Case's expression was hard to read as he addressed Walt. "How many militia members are we talking about?"

"Oh, it's hard to know." Walt scooched forward in his seat. "Ten, twelve? They don't come around very often. They make the regular people of the tribe do most of the work—what's left of them anyway—even though most of them are just as bad now. My dome is a little out of reach. I struck a deal with them years ago to fix their bio-printers and provide them with the slurry, in exchange for leaving me alone. If they threaten me, which they do on occasion, I tell them I'll just kill myself. That keeps them quiet. They like their cupcakes."

"I bet they do." I scowled. They were very delicious. "How about if I told you we could get rid of them, not only for you, but for the original tribe members who haven't been completely assimilated?"

His white bushy eyebrows rose, bunching somewhere in the middle of his forehead. "Do you mean kill them all?"

That was stating it bluntly.

"That," I hedged, "or run them out of town."

"And how would you achieve such a thing?" he scoffed. "Where would they go?"

That was a good question. I glanced at Case. "I'm sure we can come up with something."

Case grunted noncommittally.

"I'm not sure what I want," Walt confessed, rising off his chair and shuffling forward, taking his time to stand upright. "Surely not all of them are bad. We're all trying to survive in this world, are we not? Some with more violence than others."

That was a nice way of putting it.

Changing the subject for a moment, I said, "As I already said before, we came here looking for sodium alginate, a key ingredient for the cure for Plush." I had the old man's attention now. "It comes from seaweed. Does seaweed still grow here?" I couldn't help injecting some hopefulness into my words.

Walt made his way once again over to the table where the seedlings were growing. "Not in the ocean, no. And only one scientist I knew was able to grow seaweed in his lab. They sexually reproduce, you know."

No, I hadn't known.

Maisie interjected, "Alginic acid is an anionic polysaccharide found in the cell walls of seaweed, mainly kelp. Its chemical formula is six parts of carbon, eight parts of hydrogen, five parts of oxygen—"

"Stop, reader." Walt chuckled. Maisie stopped immediately. "That's a handy piece of technology you have there, boy," he said to Daze. "Protect it for all it's worth."

Daze nodded vigorously. "I will."

"Now where was I?" Walt asked.

"Seaweed sexually produces," I supplied.

"Oh, yes," Walt said. "It was incredibly lucky that some smart soul retrieved samples from the ocean before it all died out. They risked life and limb for it, among other things they collected."

"Do you know who it was that retrieved it?" I asked.

"The scientist who grew it in the lab didn't take it from the ocean himself," Walt replied. "But it doesn't matter either way. They're both gone. Seaweed and scientist. He took off with The Water Initiative."

I hadn't been expecting that, and my voice mirrored my disappointment when I asked, "Are you certain?"

"Pretty darn sure," he answered. "If he didn't, he left right around that same time and never came back."

I took a seat in order to digest this information. "Did this scientist by chance have a son who went by the name of Tandor?" Giving up wasn't in my nature. Our journey had led us here, and so far, even finding this place was an extraordinary win, but I was going to push for it all.

"He did have a son. He went by the name Teddy or some such thing. Never saw him much. They lived on the other side of town," Walt said. "Left him behind, too." The old man dipped his head. "The kid couldn't have been more than five or six at the time. Left him with a couple other scientists. None of us could ever figure out why he didn't take him along. There had to have been room. They took an entire fleet!"

Teddy had to be Tandor.

"Do you remember this scientist's name, Teddy's dad?" I asked. "When Tandor, who I think might be Teddy, left this area, he had sodium alginate powder with him. If his father was working with seaweed, the logical thought process indicates that it came from here, even if it was made a long time ago."

"The father went by the name of Candor. Well, that was his surname, I believe. After the disaster, none of that really mattered anymore. You just called yourself what you liked."

Teddy Candor had become Tandor. After all, the name Teddy didn't evoke much authority.

"The name Candor makes sense," I said, my tone coaxing. "Now we just need a location. It doesn't have to be exact. If all you have are landmarks, that's okay. We're going to need to check the place out."

Walt seemed to sink deep into thought. He began absentmindedly rearranging things on the table in front of him. After a few moments, he finally lifted his head. "The scientist Candor kept to himself. He arrived here well after we'd established a community. Some said he was running from something, but most of us were escaping from danger, so that wasn't especially peculiar. We didn't interact as a group much—only when we needed something specific, or had a need to exchange data of mutual interest. Scientists are fairly solitary beings. We prefer it that way. When Candor left to join the Flotilla, no other scientist picked up his work, as far as I know."

"That's good information to have. Thank you," I said. "But he left a child behind, and that child had something in his possession that reflected his father's work. We'll still need to hunt down his residence and check it out for ourselves."

He nodded, his expression turning mournful. "If you go there, it will be very dangerous."

One of my eyebrows quirked. "The residence itself is dangerous? Or getting there will be dangerous?"

"They've got traps set," he said. "And they're very particular about who comes into town. If they find you, they will kill you outright with no questions asked."

They sounded very welcoming. And very typical. No surprises there.

"Even the tribespeople?" I asked. "Will they react hostilely if they see us?"

"I believe they will, but I don't know them all, especially the younger ones," Walt said. "Like I said, those I used to know—who tended to be mild-mannered before—have assimilated fully into the militia lifestyle. They will follow the predilection to strike first, investigate later, which goes against every scientific code I live by. It's a shame to see it." He shook his head sadly.

Case asked Walt, "If we go investigate the scientist's residence, what are the chances we're going to find any sodium alginate there?"

"It will be slim," Walt answered. "Sodium alginate is a binding agent. It works well in the blood. It gathers things to it, detoxifying as it moves along. What do you need it for?"

"We're working on a cure for Plush," I said. "Well, not us specifically." I gestured between Case and myself. "Our scientist friend is. Along with the sodium alginate, Teddy had a quantum drive filled with formulas that had Bliss Corp logos and government stamps all over them. We think it was Candor's work."

"I was involved in many discussions about Plush over the years," Walt said. "The upgraded stuff never should've been approved for the market. Bliss Corp was in it for profit alone. It hadn't been fully tested. I shudder to think of all those people who were harmed because of greed and incompetence. Then the meteor struck, stranding all those innocent souls in limbo with no treatment."

"That's exactly why we're here," I said. "To help those people. Our friend Darby believes that he can help the infected with what's on the quantum drive and a few key ingredients, one of them being sodium alginate."

"Well, if this boy can do that, more power to him," Walt concluded. "Though the scientist in me thinks it's highly unlikely."

"He cured me," I said, feeling a little defensive about

Darby and his abilities. "If he can do that, I have faith he can help more people. He just needs the right ingredients."

Walt's mouth tumbled open. "*You* were infected with Plush? For how long?"

"Under forty-eight hours," I answered. "But that's not the point. The point is he removed it completely from my system, using the powder Teddy brought with him. If he can do that for me, he can do it for others."

Walt's eyebrows shot up. "You're a very lucky girl. He got to you before any damage could take place. But once DNA has been permanently altered, it's very hard to get it back to its original state, especially after a significant amount of time has passed. He will have a rough road ahead of him."

"Darby has said as much," I agreed. I wasn't going to share with Walt the low percentages of success Darby had quoted me. "But we came here to find what he needs. Teddy certainly believed he had access to a cure. It made him supremely confident, not to mention sloppy. He was ready to infect people with Plush to achieve his goals of taking over the city." I was going to leave out all the sex-slave stuff that came after with Hutch. No need to give the old man a heart attack.

Walt's gaze drifted somewhere over my right shoulder. "Now that we're speaking of it, if I remember correctly, the elder Candor spent many years on his work before he left. If it's there, you'll find it." He shuffled toward the bio-printer. "I will work on drawing up a map. In the meantime, let's make some more cupcakes."

My stomach growled at the prospect of more delicious food. We'd been discussing things for a while now. It was hard not to feel overwhelmed. I was supremely happy that the old man had come around and was willing to cooperate.

As Walt began to open some containers and dump them into the bio-printer, I walked over to Daze, who sat at one of the tables. "We came here hoping to find Tandor's home, and instead we find all this," I said. "What do you think?"

He glanced up at me, his expression full of innocence. "This is going to change everything, isn't it?"

Yes, kid, it surely will.

Chapter 15

"How in the hell are we supposed to run these militia members out of town? Once they figure out we're here, it'll be war." Case's voice was strained. "You heard Walt—many of the tribespeople have assimilated."

We stood outside in the drizzle, trying to come up with a decent plan that didn't include blowing up everyone we encountered from here on out.

Walt had printed up more delicious food. Something called pasta with a red sauce he'd told us was originally made with a fruit called a tomato. It'd been wondrous. The emotion I'd felt while eating something with such profound flavors had been equal to finding the ultimate salvage every minute for an entire year. I'd nearly wept, bewildered by what we'd been surviving on for so long, happy that I hadn't known this existed until now.

I hadn't been the only one overcome. Case and Daze

had had similar looks on their faces. Walt had been kind, not intruding on our private revelations.

The only one who hadn't worried about feelings was Maisie, who had informed the room that overall nutrition levels were rising to acceptable levels and had given a descriptive definition of a tomato. "Red, round, grows on a vine, and comes in many varieties."

For the first time in a very long time, my stomach felt full and satisfied. I also felt happy, which was a new emotion for me, especially coupled with food. I had never equated sustenance with joy.

It would take some getting used to.

"I don't know," I said, adjusting my helmet and flipping down my visor. It was raining a little harder now. "Running them out of town was the first thought that popped into my mind. But we're going to have to think of something else. We can't just head into town looking for Tandor's residence. That would prove deadly. We have to find a way to draw them out and keep them out until we can launch a counterattack that will work in our favor. Or sneak in. One of the two."

"Are you talking about creating a distraction?" he asked.

"Possibly." I kicked a rock on the ground, and it scuttled toward a large puddle, dropping in with a plopping sound. I was trying not to be frustrated, but protecting what we'd just found was incredibly important, and we had to go about this the right way, or we'd endanger everything. "The problem is, once they figure out it's a distraction, they'll come looking for the source, and Walt and the remaining scientists could be penalized. We can't let that happen. Things are much too valuable to risk without a solid plan."

Case ran a hand over his face.

We both knew how high the stakes were and that we had serious obstacles to conquer before we could get back to the city. Then, once we were there, we would have to make sure the unrest in the government and Port Station calmed down before we transported Walt and the other scientists—and any tribespeople who hadn't been assimilated into the militia—back.

That was, if they chose to accompany us. It would ultimately be their choice.

It would be a huge operation involving multiple crafts, and it would likely not escape the notice of the militia north of here. But we couldn't worry about that right now. We had no idea if that militia was even connected to the militia down here. We wouldn't know until we spoke to someone here who was more in the know than Walt, and doing so would expose us.

Thinking about all the logistics was making my head ache. But I was committed. I'd do whatever it took.

Case brushed past me, moving around the side of the dome. I followed.

He turned abruptly, and I stopped just before I plowed into his back. "I believe Walt when he told us they're not all bad," Case said. The outskirt had firsthand experience with the power-hungry militia and, subsequently, their deaths. This couldn't be easy for him. "But that doesn't mean people won't be killed." I'd just been thinking the same thing. "The only option I can see is we figure out who's a threat and who's not. We eliminate the threats and make a deal with those remaining. It's the only way to achieve our goals."

"That could work," I replied. "But in order to do that, we have to isolate a few and get them to talk."

"Walt has to know at least some names and possible locations of those he would deem good," Case said. "You pay attention to that stuff when your life is constantly on the line. That's a start."

"He says he makes slurry for them," I said. "He said the militia makes the tribespeople pick it up. They must have a schedule. How long can a bucket of slurry last? I'm thinking a week, tops. Let's head back in, ask him when the next delivery is, and we wait." It would delay getting back to the city, but I could see no other choice.

"We should also check out the dome next door," Case said, his body language agitated as he shifted back and forth. We were both on edge. "If Walt's residence is that expansive, the next one should be equally as big. Who knows what that Ronston guy left in there?"

"Agreed." I ran a hand along the smooth surface of Walt's dome. The dirt had to have been mixed with concrete, or another material that hardened to stone. "I wish we could get a message to Bender, Lockland, and Darby. Finding all this is going to change the scope of our mission and our lives going forward. It's a game changer, and it would be a benefit to have them down here. With more power, overcoming this militia wouldn't be difficult at all."

"The militia likely has radio frequency set up, but nothing that would travel that far," Case said.

"I know," I said. "It's wishful thinking." I glanced over Case's shoulder at the rolling dunes. "If we're planning to stay here for at least a few days, we're going to need supplies. I'll head back to Seven and get our packs. You go inside and talk to Walt about the slurry pickup schedule. When I return, we can decide what to do." I didn't wait for a response. We both needed to think on our own. We'd been tossing things back and forth for at least fifteen minutes.

I headed toward the sea, up and over rolling dunes.

After trudging across four small hills, I spotted Seven. She was easy to spot, because the reflective cloth had blown completely away, nowhere to be seen, at least from here. "Damn," I muttered. I'd have to find a better way to secure it. After I found the cloth. I hoped it hadn't blown too close to the sea.

When I was approximately thirty meters from the craft, I detected movement out of the corner of my eye. I dropped instantly, my palms splayed in front of me in the scrub to hold my balance, my back and head low.

Unlucky for me, there weren't a lot of places to go undetected out here.

I lifted my head and squinted.

Down on the beach, a pair of figures walked in the

sand, occasionally bending over to pick something up as they moved unsuspectingly toward Seven. "Shit," I said. It seemed they hadn't spotted the craft yet, judging by their casual movements. She was parked over a short incline.

It was possible they would pass without seeing her, but not probable.

Not even five minutes later, the reflective cloth I hadn't been able to spot caught a gust of wind and flew up over the hill like a gigantic, highly visible parachute. You'd have to be blind not to see it.

I watched their body movements as they caught sight of it. They glanced at each other before hurrying toward the cloth, which had dipped down behind another incline and out of my sight.

Capturing people to question this soon hadn't been the plan, but it was now.

There was no other choice. Once they reached the craft, they'd radio for help, if they didn't decide to do it sooner.

The most logical option would be to wait for them to approach the craft and take them by surprise. But in order to do that, I had to get closer without being seen.

I took my chances while they were distracted by the cloth, which had billowed back into view. Staying as low as possible, I rushed toward Seven and took cover beside her, crouching by the passenger door, my hands braced against her metal sides, my head ducked beneath the windows.

Thankfully, my utility bag was secured at my waist. I unzipped it and withdrew a pair of macro-glasses. I popped my visor and secured them over my eyes.

I brought my head up a little over the hood. The lenses made it seem like the two people were right in front of me. A man and a woman—no, a boy and a girl, early twenties, if that. Even though they were both helmeted, it was clear they were young, which was a bonus. They were still distracted trying to get the cloth under control. Both were armed and wore green uniforms typical of a militia. Uniforms helped separate people by rank and affiliation. It also helped someone like me know who I was dealing with. Thanks, uniforms.

Seven was bulky enough to give me ample cover. I just had to make sure they didn't spot me before I was ready. They would definitely come this way, weapons drawn, to investigate where the cloth had come from. That was what I would do.

Holding the advantage once they arrived was important. Inside my utility bag I had some nano-carbon cubes, which I used to power my Gem. They would do nicely as a distraction.

As the pair came closer, I calculated the best time to make my move. I saw the moment they noticed Seven. The boy grabbed the girl by the arm, gesturing frantically. Not exactly subtle.

They plowed ahead, rushing faster. The boy had the cloth wadded up under his arm. Their movements betrayed their youth even more. Someone seasoned would've found cover and investigated from a distance.

I slid to the back of the craft, peeking through Seven's rear window, my head so low only my eyes were above the line. They both had their weapons out, as expected. As they maneuvered closer, I got a better look. The girl's arm was steadier than the boy's, and he kept giving her furtive glances.

She was in charge.

I would focus my attention, and my Gem, on her. Once they were within five meters, I flicked my wrist, sending a few nano-carbon cubes flying over the top of Seven. There was only a one-in-five chance that all the cubes would explode. The ground wasn't that firm, and the cubes needed a jolt of force to explode.

I'd sent six, hoping that at least one would cooperate.

A moment later, two small explosions, nothing more than cracks in the air, were followed by small blinks of light.

They were enough.

The pair turned toward the threat, weapons up.

I leaped out, my Gem in one hand, my taser in the other. "Stay right there and don't turn toward me if you want to live." I issued the warning in my sternest tone, hoping they would comply.

As predicted, the boy did as I asked, but the girl began to pivot.

I depressed the trigger of my Gem lightly, letting up immediately, sending a short blast at the ground a meter from her feet. It made her jump. "Don't move," I reiterated. This time, she stayed still. I edged closer. "If you try anything"—I came around in front of them, my Gem barrel aimed at neck level on the boy—"I hit him first, understand?" I had her attention now.

She gave me a look like she wanted to sever my head from my shoulders and present it to me on a titanium tray. A slow nod followed.

"Get on your knees and put your weapons down," I ordered. When they didn't comply quickly enough, I let another blast fly, this one in front of the boy. He visibly blanched, dropping the reflective cloth and his weapon, which was a tired-looking Blaster. The girl had an ample-looking laser. After a moment, she tossed it in front of her.

Moving forward, I kicked the weapons away as carefully as I could. Guns in our world were always unstable. "Place your hands on your heads." I didn't want them to reach for anything in their pockets. The girl rolled her eyes at me. "What?" I scoffed. "You don't think I know you're carrying more weapons? You're militia, aren't you? Your uniforms say you are."

"Yes, we're militia," she spat. "You think you're tough shit for getting us, but you're gonna be real sorry when the others find you." She spoke with a slight pidgin accent, but not enough to have a problem understanding her.

"I'm sure I'm *gonna* be real sorry," I retorted. "That is, if your people can get to me before I get to them." I circled behind them, holstering my guns, drawing out one of the two cuffs I had in my jacket pocket. I clasped the girl's hands behind her back first and secured them, then the boy's. The cuff was made of thin, flexible wire coated in pliable aluminum. Once the nodes were connected, a continuous current of electricity flowed through them, generated by a small chemical reaction. As long as the current stayed intact, it was grounded. If either of them tried to break their restraints, they would be electrocuted. "You know what these are, don't you? They're electro-cuffs, e-cuffs for short." I directed my commentary between them. "Don't try to take them off. If you do, you'll fry." *Frying* was a bit extreme, as these weren't military grade, but they didn't have to know that.

If they broke the connection, the worst that would happen was they'd be knocked out for a minute or two. That would be enough time for me to get them back under control.

"Please don't hurt us," the boy pleaded.

"I'm not planning on it," I said, heading back to stand in front of them. "If you cooperate by answering my questions, you'll survive, no problem." I hadn't planned on admitting as much so soon, but lying to these two kids seemed counterproductive. If the militia had arrived five or six years ago, these two would've been young teenagers, probably original tribespeople. They'd had no choice but to join the militia.

I couldn't necessarily blame them for their actions. At least not yet.

The girl spat on the ground as I patted them both down, looking for additional weapons and a communication device and not finding any. "They're going to find us, and when they do, you're gonna die real slow."

I crouched next to her. "Why don't you have any other defenses or tech on you—"

"What's going on?" Case called as he shot over the hill and spotted us. His weapon was drawn. "I heard blasts."

I stood, facing him, hands on my hips. "Those were nano-carbon cubes," I said matter-of-factly. "I needed a distraction. I found these two walking along the beach. I waited for them to approach before I set off the charges. They're admitted militia, and as far as I can tell after a cursory search, they don't have any other weapons or a tech phone on them, which I'm thinking is a little unusual. The girl's in charge. My guess is they were on patrol. We might have gone without notice, but the reflective cloth got loose." I walked behind the girl and searched one more time to be sure I hadn't missed anything.

She thrust backward, showing her irritation. It was clear she hadn't encountered much trouble before, or she wouldn't have been so gutsy.

"They're going to cut you real bad," she declared as I finished up.

"So you've been telling me." I withdrew a small square box from a lower pocket in her pants. It was small and thin, no more than three centimeters thick, made out of some kind of shiny metal I wasn't familiar with.

"Don't go and touch that!" she yelled. "You'll be sorry."

"I'll take my chances."

I lifted the lid.

Chapter 16

Scattered inside the box was a pile of chipped, white fragments I couldn't identify. "What are these?" I asked. The girl was tight-lipped, livid that I was messing with her stuff. I held it out to Case. "Do you know what these are?"

He took a look and shrugged. "No, but Walt will. Bring them inside. Somebody's going to miss these two soon, and it's better if we're not out in the open when they do." He holstered his gun and took the boy by the arm, hauling him up, grabbing the reflective cloth with his other hand.

I did the same with the girl after I put the box in my utility bag. She continued to buck me. I had no choice but to curb her behavior before it got out of control. She had to understand who was in charge. And, spoiler, it wasn't her. My fingers tightened on her forearm as we walked. "I get that you're tough," I murmured. "I am, too. And in a world dominated by men, a woman has to be ten times tougher than any man to be taken seriously. But you're not going to win this battle. Not cooperating is only going to make things worse."

"You don't know anything, *slippy*," she sneered.

Slippy must be a derogatory term, one I'd never heard before. I didn't mind being called slippy.

I jostled her over a particularly bumpy patch of ground, and when she began to fall, I yanked her back up, pressing her tightly against my chest, forcing her head back uncomfortably. This was the kind of language she knew, and unlucky for her, I was well versed in it. "You're going to cooperate one way or another," I purred in her ear. "If you don't, I drug you. And once your body is lifeless, we can do anything we like to it. Do you hear me? Drop the attitude." She began to struggle in earnest, so I tried another tactic. "Okay, if you prefer, we can torture your friend instead." She stilled immediately. The boy was her weakness, and she cared nothing for herself. Her history had to be riddled with abuse, and I felt like an asshole for playing on that and wished this could go another way. But our agenda now was too damn important, and she had to *believe* we were capable of doing something awful—at least until we received the information we needed. Letting up on the pressure, I said, "If you cooperate, I give you my word that nothing happens to the boy. You step out of line, he gets a dagger in the thigh, and that's just the beginning." I released my tight hold on her, and she stumbled forward, my hand still gripped around her arm.

She straightened and began to walk without protest.

At the dome, Case ushered us inside without preamble. He went first, then the boy, then the girl, then me. Walt stood slowly as we entered. Daze came forward, eyes alert and curious, darting back and forth as he tried to deduce what had happened.

Before any of us could speak, Maisie declared, "I detect six humans within five meters. Heart rate on new female elevated. Hydration required. Nutrition inadequate."

The girl scowled, and I chuckled. "At least I'm not the only one. Maisie clearly has an affinity for women."

Maisie said, "Females have superior brain recall and immune systems. They can create new life—"

"That's enough, Maisie. But thanks for the lesson," I said as I turned to Walt. "I found these two walking by the sea. I had no choice but to take them once they discovered our craft. Case and I are going to question them and figure out who the sympathizers are in the tribe. Do they look familiar?"

While we waited for an answer, Case forced them both to sit, their hands still bound behind their backs. The girl spoke before Walt could respond. "I've heard of you, old man," she said. "They protect you real good. You give us food sometimes."

Walt turned to me. "I've never seen these two before." His bushy eyebrows went up. "But if they think I feed them only sometimes, rather than all the time, they are not in the know. The militia has a strict ranking system. They must be at the bottom."

The girl took offense at Walt's assessment of them. "We aren't at the bottom," she spat. "We're in the middle. There's at least ten below us."

Rank mattered. Good to know.

"What's your name?" I asked, moving to stand in front of her. When she acted like she wasn't going to answer, I slid my Gem out slowly. "I asked your name."

"Gia." Her chin came jutting out in a Daze-worthy move. She tipped her head toward the boy. "He's Knox."

Before I could say anything, Daze strode forward purposefully, stopping in front of her. "They're not going to hurt you," he said, his voice full of emotion. "I'm a street kid, and they saved my life. All you need to do is cooperate, and you'll be okay."

I placed a hand on Daze's shoulder, giving it a small squeeze. "What he means is, if you cooperate, we won't hurt you. If you don't, we will." Daze's heart was in the right place, but he got the hint.

If Gia truly thought we weren't going to hurt her, she'd never cooperate.

The kid cleared his throat. "Yeah, what I meant was, if you cooperate, you'll be fine. But Holly"—he gestured to me—"shot her laser through this guy and smoked him a couple days ago. Then she gave this other guy a radium ball, and he started bleeding from the mouth and his skin started sliding off." Had Dill's skin slid off? I hadn't known that, likely because I'd been busy fighting off the insane effects of Plush. "Then this other guy—"

I applied a small amount of pressure to Daze's shoulder again, and he stopped. He had more than redeemed himself. The girl and the boy were rapt by his revelations, their eyes so wide white showed all the way around. My previous actions had sounded even more grisly coming from the kid in such a casual tone.

Using their reactions as my guide, I drew up a chair and sat backward, resting my arms across the top of the back, my Gem still out. Affecting a conversational tone, I started, "Gia and Knox, do you see what's around you? You know where we are?"

They both tore their eyes off of Daze and glanced around, their gazes lingering on the green plants, as I'd suspected.

Knox spoke first. "I've heard about this place. You're one of the scientists," he said to Walt. "The one who lives a day away." That was good information. The rest of the inhabitants were a day's walk from here. "They say you, out of all of them, are the most important."

"That's good," I told Knox, coaxing his gaze back to mine, giving him a warm smile. "Everything you see in here is important and needs to be protected at all costs." I'd emphasized the last few words. "Do you understand what I'm saying?"

Gia's expression changed quickly, and it appeared like she was about to spit on the ground in front of her. "It means you want to take our stuff," she snarled.

"We're not going to let you. We'll fight you before—"

Case placed both hands on her shoulders to keep her still. At the contact, she jumped like she'd been struck by an electrical pulse.

No one ever got used to abuse, no matter how much they tried to harden themselves against it. My tone was quiet as I addressed her. "We're not going to leave the tribe with nothing," I replied, careful to use the word *tribe* instead of *militia*. "Whoever cooperates will be taken care of." I decided to change my line of questioning. "Do you want to have a child someday?" It was an extremely intimate question, and her expression showed exactly what she thought of me asking her something so personal. "It's a fair question," I argued. "Are you planning on having a family?"

"Maybe," she muttered, her eyes darting to the boy, then away as her cheeks tinted red.

They were lovers.

"Do you want that child to have a good life? Better than yours?" I asked. It was a rhetorical question—of course she did.

"They will have a good life," she countered stubbornly. "We live here with this stuff. We have food and medicine, everything we need."

I gestured to Walt. "Does this man look young to you? Does he look like he's going to survive to see your children grow up?"

Before Gia could reply, Knox stood abruptly, taking us all by surprise.

Case was on him in the next instant, grabbing him

by the shoulders. "I didn't mean any harm," Knox sputtered. "We will cooperate. We will do whatever you want. We want a better life than this one! Living here, under the militia, is awful."

Gia looked as if she was trying to decide whether to punch him or protect him.

"Don't move," I warned, giving her a look. "If you do anything, I'll shoot him in the leg." I waved my Gem in the air. "It's not a knife, and the laser will hurt more. It might even kill him." I nodded to Case. "Let him go. Let's hear what he has to say."

Case dropped his hold and took a step back. "We're already in trouble," Knox started. "We were supposed to be on patrol, but we decided to just keep walking." He darted a glance at Gia, who refused to look at him. "We weren't going back. We didn't care where we got to, just as long as it wasn't back there."

Now we were getting someplace.

I got off my chair and paced toward him, making sure I proceeded slowly. "Do they hurt you? Who runs things? Tell us everything, and we'll help you. We'll remove the threat and take you back to the city with us." My voice stressed what was at stake. "You two can start a new life together. Your children will be able to grow and flourish." Hopefully. But from what Knox was saying, life here wasn't great, so anything would be a step up.

Maisie's voice broke in. "I detect six humans within five meters and two humans within forty meters."

Not at all welcome information.

Chapter 17

I turned to Walt. "When they come to you, do they come from the sea or inland?"

He sputtered nervously, "They come from inland. There's a path. I believe they only have one craft these days. It's not very reliable. A few months ago, all their crafts were taken. Most of the time they walk, or they only take the craft part of the way."

"If we lock the door, will they stay outside?" I asked. "Even if you don't choose to answer it?"

The old man shook his head. "No, they will persist until I open it. They are in possession of explosives that will blast through my door." That wasn't a risk I was willing to take.

"Is there a place we can take cover within the dome?" Case asked.

"Yes, yes, of course." Walt moved toward a hatch set in the ground. "This is where I keep my specimens that need to remain at a constant temperature."

I grabbed Daze by the arm, pulling him close, murmuring, "Once we get down there, I'm going to need you to help keep the two of them quiet. You go first and scout it out." The kid nodded once and took off, helping Walt hoist the door in the floor, scampering down the moment it was clear. I addressed Case. "If they're arriving from inland, there's a good chance they won't spot Seven, even without the reflective cloth. There are enough hills to block her from sight, assuming they don't fly high enough. My guess is they're coming to check up on these two." I gestured at Gia and Knox, who stood in front of Case, their hands still secured behind their backs. "If Walt can convince them he hasn't seen them, there shouldn't be any issues, and hopefully, they'll leave." I looked at Walt, who was breathing heavily from the effort of getting the door open. He must not use that space very often. "We'll be listening. If it sounds like there's going to be trouble, we will come to your aid. Tell them, with certainty, that you haven't seen these two. Can you do that?"

Case maneuvered the boy and girl forward and down the short steps.

When Walt didn't answer my question, I gently grabbed his arm, tugging him toward his sleeping pallet. "Listen, deception can be difficult, but I know you can do this. If you pretend you've been asleep, you can act flustered without it seeming unnatural. When you turn the lights on, tell them you haven't seen anyone. If they don't believe you, threaten them by withholding slurry. Can you do that?" We stood next to his pallet.

He met my gaze, his eyes a little blurred. "Yes, I think so."

"Good." I pressed him down on his bed, and he went willingly. "Remember, we will be listening and will come to your aid if necessary. Where are the light switches?"

A bony arm came up, indicating a place next to the main set of stairs. I walked over, punching my shoulder light on so I could see once it was dark. "Lie back on the pallet." He did as I asked. "Everything's going to be fine." I doused the lights, flipping multiple switches, and made my way over to the hatch.

As I went, I opened my utility bag and drew out a dart. I was going to need it.

Walt's voice wavered slightly as he said, "They won't hurt me. I'm sure of it. What I provide them is much too valuable."

Grabbing on to the door handle as I descended underground, I replied, "I'm sure they won't, but if it sounds like they're going to change their minds, we will intervene. You're not dying today, old man."

Once I was down, I glanced around the small space.

It was nothing more than a storage compartment. Rickety shelves stacked with glass jars lined one wall, their contents murky. Case had Gia and Knox on the floor, backs against the only available, dirty wall. I squatted in front of them, directing my gaze pointedly at Knox. "Will she try to alert them that we're here?" I asked, my voice low as I rolled the dart between my fingers, unseen by either of them. The only thing illuminating the space was my shoulder light.

Knox darted a glance at her, unsure whether to answer. I gave him a look that said I wasn't kidding around. "I don't…I'm not sure…"

"That's okay," I told him. "I was only asking out of courtesy. I'm not willing to take any chances." Before either of them had time to process what I'd said, I brought the dart up and inserted it into Gia's thigh, punching it quickly through her pants. She gaped at me, her expression horrified, like I was killing her. "This is just temporary," I murmured. "I know you think it's the right choice to alert your tribe of any danger. But we're not here to harm you. You'll wake in about an hour, after they're gone. You might have a touch of a headache, but nothing more." She slumped to the side, onto Knox, her eyes fluttering shut. He took her weight willingly, leaning his head against hers sweetly. I turned my attention on him, making sure he was looking at me so he'd understand. "If you so much as cough, you won't be getting a tranq dart," I told him in a low whisper. "And it will also mean that we'll have to kill the men upstairs. Do you understand? Make a sound, and they die." He nodded, fear in his eyes. I was satisfied.

Standing, I turned toward Case, who was positioned right below the hatch, listening. Daze had taken a seat next to the shelves.

Before I could say anything, Daze asked, "She's going to wake up, right?"

"What do you think?"

"I think she's going to wake up," he said decisively, with a quick nod.

"She'll wake up if she doesn't have an allergic reaction to whatever's in that dart," I clarified. "It needed to be done, Daze. She's too unpredictable, and we have to protect what's upstairs at all costs."

"I know," he said, his voice solemn and full of understanding.

"You're going to have to make sure Maisie doesn't speak while we're down here," I told him. "Can you do that?" His face went slack as he began to pat his pockets frantically. Oh, no. "Please tell me you have the egg on you."

"I'm sorry, Holly." His voice broke. "I left it upstairs, on the table near the plants."

I addressed Case. "Do you think if Maisie speaks, it will alarm them?"

"Hard to know," he answered. "Walt has a lot of tech up there. They can't know everything he has."

"That's true," I said. "But what if she says something that gives us away? Like stating how many humans are in the room? That's her favorite line." I started up the short flight of steps, my palm bracing against the hatch. It came up easily. "It'll be safer if I go get her. I'm pretty sure I can grab her and be back down here before they arrive."

"What is it?" Walt sputtered as I entered the room.

"We left the status reader here," I whispered. "She's unpredictable, and I don't want anything giving us away."

"Good idea," Walt answered as I dropped my visor down and turned off my shoulder light as a precautionary move. There was barely enough ambient light for me to see via infrared, but I managed. I headed toward the plant table. "LiveBot software is quite adaptable," the old man said, "and based on what she's learned so far, she could say anything. She will have to be taught when to speak and when not to, but it will take some time. She's too smart for her own good."

"Good to know," I muttered. Once I was at the table, I searched around, but didn't see the egg. "Maisie, where are you?"

Maisie's lights exploded from two tables over. "I am located north of you. I detect two humans upon us with hydrogen weapons—"

"Stop," I commanded as I rushed over and swiped her up just as the door above us shuddered open. I dove behind the table in front of me, bringing the egg up to my lips, and in a harsh whisper said, "So help me, Maisie, if you speak again before I tell you to, I will crush you into a million pieces." Her lights zipped around. "And no more lights." They snapped off immediately.

I took that as a good sign that she would follow my commands and shoved her into my pocket.

Two men were murmuring above. Then a voice

shouted, "We're coming down, old man! If you retaliate, we will kill you! So no funny stuff."

Two bodies began to descend into the darkness. I was fairly secure behind this table, if they didn't lean over the top. I wasn't worried about them killing me before I could defend myself. I was worried about the repercussions of them not returning to their people before we had a solid plan in place.

"I was asleep," Walt croaked as he sat up. "Hit the lights when you get down here. They are next to the stairs." It seemed Walt was a pro at feigning surprise.

"What are you doing sleeping during the day?" a male voice said as the lights came on. "Get the hell out of bed. We're almost out of slurry. You should be working hard instead of sleeping." His voice held a pidgin accent similar to that of the boy and the girl. He must've been born here and not an original militia member. But that was just a hypothesis. I'd have to wait and see. Walt wasn't moving fast enough, his legs just coming over the side of the pallet. I watched as one of the men strode over and grabbed Walt by the arm, dragging him forward, causing him to stumble. "Hurry up, old man."

These two were on edge.

There was a distinct possibility they'd spotted Seven. I gritted my teeth, my hand on my Gem as I watched the guy manhandle Walt. I ached to use my weapon, even to give them a warning, but doing so wouldn't work to our advantage. It was all about the advantage.

The other man, who'd come in behind the first, moved through the dome methodically, taking everything in. He was the one to look out for.

"I have the new slurry you requested, but it's not here," Walt protested. "I already took it to the usual meeting place."

The new man spoke for the first time. "We didn't come in that way," he said in perfect English, no hint of pidgin. "We came by craft."

Walt had said the tribe's only craft wasn't reliable. If they'd been forced to take it all the way out here, they were likely on the hunt for Gia and Knox, but my guess was they'd spotted Seven on the way in and were trying to figure out what to do. That would explain their hostile attitudes. They would try to coax some answers out of Walt, before getting physical.

At least, that's what I'd do.

Both men wore helmets and the same green uniforms as Gia and Knox, marking them clearly as militia. They also had full waist holsters for their weapons—which they hadn't drawn—with several compartments attached to the belt that probably held small hydro-bombs, which Maisie had indicated they had.

My senses were heightened, and I knew Case's were, too. If one of them opened the hatch, they'd get a Pulse bullet in the face.

"We're going to need some information from you," the first man said. He stood next to Walt in front of the bio-printer. He was definitely more nervous than the other one, his voice quaking in anger, or maybe fear. If I'd had to guess, I would have said he hadn't had to deal with any surprises since the militia arrived. "If you answer truthfully, we won't hurt you."

The other guy stopped walking, interjecting, "We're looking for two of our members." His voice held an edge. No fear. "Have they been out this way?"

They're trying to bait him. They know about Seven.

As quietly as I could, I drew my Gem.

"I haven't seen anyone," Walt said, his voice breaking slightly at the end.

Damn.

The man with no fear took a step toward Walt. "Are you sure about that, old man? We find you here sleeping in the middle of the day, and now you're looking a little panicked. If you're lying, it won't end well for you. We know you bring us benefit, but we protect our own first. There are two more of you. I'm sure they can figure out what you've got going on here." He waved a hand in front of the bio-printing machine.

Walt sputtered, "You're…you're hardly an authority on my sleeping habits." His voice lost its shake. *Go, Walt!* "I often take a nap at midday. I find it rejuvenates me. My work is difficult and arduous, something you couldn't possibly understand. And, no, I haven't seen a single soul. If they came out here with the intent to find me, you might want to try the other dome, because they're certainly not here."

The man slowly removed his weapon from its holster.

Shit.

It was a large gun with a steel frame. I wasn't sure what it shot, but it wasn't a laser. My fingers curled around my Gem, which was positioned next to my thigh.

Looked like things were going to escalate quickly from here.

The man moved forward, raising the gun, positioning it at Walt's temple. "We know you're hiding them," he said. "Admit it."

The other, aggressive man was bolstered by his pal. "Yeah, admit it," he echoed. Then, without warning, he whipped his arm back and punched Walt in the stomach.

The old man doubled over with a loud *whoosh,* wrapping his frail arms around his middle as he gasped for breath.

Both men had their backs to me. I stood soundlessly, easing my HydroSol air gun out of its holster with my left hand, my right already positioned outward. A bullet from this would create an air bubble that would blow up the heart.

Once Walt was standing mostly upright again, the contemplative guy said, "We don't want to kill you, but we really need those two back. And that's not even accounting for the craft sitting out by the dunes. What are you hiding from us, old man? I'm going to give you five seconds to answer before I put a hole—"

"Me." My voice was icy. "He's hiding me." My guns were leveled, one on each man, as I made my way out from behind the table.

Both men reacted predictably, turning quickly, their arms swinging wide. I edged to the right, needing them positioned so that their backs were to the hatch. They obliged, moving their arms to follow me.

"Who the hell are you?" the belligerent man shouted. "What have you done with our militia members?"

"Your members are safe," I assured him. "We didn't take them. Our paths just happened to cross. But the way I see it, everything happens for a reason. Ever heard of karma?" A look of confusion passed over each man's face.

Very slowly, the calmer of the two swung his gun back toward Walt.

He knew what I was willing to protect, and it wasn't myself.

I would've been nervous had I not known what was lurking behind him, opening the hatch as we spoke. This man could feasibly kill Walt before I could kill him, and he knew it. He thought he had the upper hand.

He thought wrong.

Chapter 18

"I'll kill him, then I'll destroy everything in here. All the stuff you want," the man threatened calmly. "Return our members to us, and no one has to die." He could've ended with *right now*. But it was implied.

When I encountered men who didn't know me, most of the time they figured that because I was female, I was gullible, a pushover, or not gritty enough to make tough choices. I'd been known to play this angle up from time to time.

This was one of those times.

To make it seem more legitimate, I added a small tremor to my hands, allowing my weapons to shake. "Please don't kill him," I implored, cracking my voice at the end. "He's too valuable. I'll do *anything*."

The confident man took a bold step forward, his gun still trained on Walt. I could read in his face that all the other plausible ideas of who I was when I first drew my weapons were falling by the wayside as he took my new words and cowering demeanor and assimilated them into the situation.

"Get down on your knees," he ordered, testing me. Then he nodded to the other man. "Strap the old man up in a chair until we finish this. We'll deal with him later."

I hesitated for a few seconds before complying. It was enough for him to take a step toward me, swinging his gun on me. "I said get on your knees."

Bringing my arms up into a surrender pose, I began to ease downward. "Okay, I'm going," I said. "But you promised not to hurt him. You have to keep your—"

"Quiet," he snarled as he stormed toward me. "Drop your weapons." This one was fond of violence. His mouth quirked in a smile at the prospect of my not acquiescing. He had me where he wanted me. I had submitted.

I eased my guns onto the ground.

"Who are you?" he demanded. When I didn't answer, he stopped in front of me, swinging his fist toward my face, about to teach me a lesson.

At the last possible moment, I grabbed hold of his wrist and stood in a rush, using the momentum to wrench his arm toward me, giving him a solid headbutt. As he recoiled, I kicked the gun from his other hand and spun him around, holding him secure with his forearm cocked behind his back, my Gem at his temple.

I wished I could see his face as he realized what had been waiting behind him.

He gasped audibly in the face of Case's pulse gun, which was mere centimeters from his left eye. Case's other weapon was trained on the militia man who stood, his mouth agape, in front of Walt.

The guy I was holding immediately began to struggle. "You're not going to want to do that." I gripped his arm tighter. "First, I break this, and then it gets worse from there. How many in your militia?"

"Fuck you," he ground out. I wasn't surprised he was refusing to cooperate. It was his pal we would get information from, not him.

Case stalked toward the other guy, obviously having heard the entire interaction and coming to the same conclusion. "Sit," he commanded the man. When he still stood there looking unsure, Case cracked the butt of his weapon across the top of his head.

"Ow!" the guy whined, grabbing his head as he sat with a thump next to Walt.

"We want information," Case told both men, then addressed the guy in the chair. "And you're the one who's going to give it to us."

"The hell I am—" Case used his fist this time, crashing it into his jaw. The powerful blow sent the guy flying backward to sprawl on the ground. Case was over him a moment later, a large boot settled on his chest.

"See that?" I told the guy. "If you don't cooperate, you die, and your friend dies." It was important to show force now, to ultimately get them to answer our questions.

"You think I care?" he snarled. "It's you two who are dying. And it's going to be painful. We specialize in that around here."

Unsurprising. "I bet. You also specialize in beating women, don't you? That's why it was so easy for you to believe I was frail and useless. I bet it kills you to be restrained so easily by a female." Predictably, he started to squirm, giving me no choice but to do as I'd threatened.

I broke the bone cleanly, knowing where to apply the greatest amount of pressure.

He screamed, one of his legs giving out beneath him. He was heavy, but I had him braced against my shoulder. Forcing him to stand, still holding on to the broken limb, I whispered, "I warned you what was going to happen. Apparently, you weren't listening."

Across the room, Case ordered the other guy to confess. "How many in your militia?"

Before the man could answer, a noise came from the back of the room.

Knox stumbled out of the hatch, Daze trailing behind him. The kid had a cut on his cheek, a line of blood rolling down his face like an angry tear. There'd been a skirmish. I swore under my breath.

"I'll tell you," Knox said, breathing heavily from his efforts. His hands were still secured behind him, but his clothes were ripped. Daze had tried to restrain him, which made me proud. "There are twenty-nine of us. Six are under the age of eighteen. These two"—he nodded at both men—"report to two others above them. If they go missing, there will be no negotiation. They will bomb you and be done with it."

"Thank you, Knox," I said. "But we weren't under the impression there would be any negotiation once it got to this point." The guy I held whimpered in pain, because as I spoke, his body was jostled. "We're committed now."

Knox appeared confused for a moment. Then he nodded, understanding that there was no going back for any of us. He'd chosen his side. He leaned his head toward Case's captive. "That's Tim, and he'll want you dead no matter what happens." He reluctantly glanced my way. He was fearful of the man I held, my Gem still locked at his temple. That told me all I needed to know. "That's Curtis, and he will pretend to negotiate and then kill you at the first opportunity."

The guy in my arms stopped moaning. "He's right. You better kill us, bitch. I'm coming for you the moment—"

I struck him across the head with my Gem.

He crumpled against me, and I slid him to the ground, stepping over his body, shaking my head. I glanced at Case, who still had his boot on the other man's chest. "How do you want to work this?" I asked. Case appeared apprehensive for a moment. Almost as if he was trying to figure out what he thought *I* wanted to do, not what he would do.

Finally, he answered, "We keep them alive until we assess the situation. Knox can provide us with a map of the town and who the key resistance players will be.

There are at least six children, and they have to be considered." He was correct on all counts.

"It's going to take both of us to take on the militia," I said. "That means we have to leave Daze and Knox in charge of things here."

Case glanced between the two men. "We'll need to ensure they're tied securely."

Walt ambled forward. "I might have something to keep them docile while you're away."

I peered at the old man as he made his way to a table, reaching to open a drawer underneath. He didn't look any worse for the wear from his encounter. In fact, he appeared energized.

He withdrew a bunch of beakers and jars filled with different-colored liquids, setting them on the counter. Then he held one up to the light and swirled it around. It had a blue tint to it. "I've been perfecting this for a long while now." He looked pleased.

"What does it do?" I came forward, squinting into the jar. "Are those teeth?"

He laughed good-naturedly. "No, no. Those are shell fragments. The outer covering of crustaceans that inhabited the seas long ago. They help stabilize the chemical compounds."

I gazed closer, remembering Gia's box in my pocket. I drew it out and lifted the lid, shaking the contents around. Walt peered into it as well. "Are these shells?"

"Why, yes, they are," he replied. "I have the tribe pick them up for me, in exchange for the slurry."

I turned around, glancing at Knox. "You were coming here, weren't you?" I asked. "You were collecting shells and were coming here to ask Walt for help. Did you think he could aid you?"

Knox immediately shuffled his feet, his gaze landing on Curtis, who was still out cold, his broken arm positioned at an odd angle. His expression went from uncomfortable to angry in less than a second. He met my stare, drawing himself up. "We were going to ask the old man if he had something that would take someone out."

"Poison?" I asked. "Or a weapon?"

Knox shrugged. "Anything that couldn't be identified. Poison or drugs. Something like that."

My gaze darted to where Knox had gestured at the blue solution in Walt's hand. "What is that?" I asked Walt.

"It doesn't kill," Walt said. "It just makes the person more…amiable. But I do possess what the child is referring to. I would never resort to using it without just cause, however."

I turned back to Knox. "How bad is it that you needed to come here to find a means to kill someone? Be honest with me. I need to know what we're up against."

"Things have always been bad, but manageable, I guess." He didn't sound convinced, and I didn't blame him. Bad was always bad. Manageable was a state of mind that kept you sane. "Recently, the leaders of our militia have been in negotiations with another group north of here. They are really…*nasty.*" He'd uttered the last word on a breath as he crossed his arms, likely to keep himself steady. "When they first came here, they killed two people just to prove a point. And they did it—with knives. Small ones. If Jorgen, our leader, agrees to merge with them, our lives will become infinitely worse." He had to be talking about the militia we'd flown over in what used to be South Carolina. They were definitely staking their claim. "Me and Gia…won't live through it."

"Militias like the one we're talking about don't usually ask for permission to take over," I said. "Why is there any negotiation at all?"

"Jorgen and a few others know those guys," he said. "The militia said they were giving us a 'courtesy' by asking. But we all know it's just a matter of time."

The man underneath Case's foot began to struggle. Tim had been quiet up until now, probably too scared to make a fuss, knowing we'd retaliate with force. "He's not telling the truth," Tim whined. "We'll all be better off with them! They provide more protection."

From who? And did he really believe that? Of course he did.

"And women," Tim went on. "They have more than us. That bitch he's with is one of only five we have, not including children. There's no way for us to procreate."

Procreate was a lie. These assholes didn't care about making more people. They didn't have enough women to rape. Five out of twenty-nine.

My heart skipped a beat for Gia.

I met Knox's eyes. They said it all. Guilt, remorse, love, and sadness flitted over his features in the time it took to blink.

He focused a hard gaze on the floor in front of him.

Disgust flowed through my body. I cursed this world. Why did humans have to be so cruel?

A loud *oof* sounded from my left.

I glanced over to see that Tim was now unconscious. Good. The bastard was lucky he wasn't dead. I turned to Walt. "Go ahead and give the two guys who are out cold that stuff, and we'll tie them up." I nodded to the blue solution he'd set back on the table. Then I addressed Knox. "I need names and descriptions of all the people who live here. Those who you consider good and those who will cause the most problems, and I need it quickly. We've already wasted enough time. People will come looking for these two sooner than later."

Knox appeared frightened, his face crumpling.

"What is it?" I asked.

"There's only a handful of people who are good," he replied.

"And?"

"It won't be enough."

"Enough for what?"

"To defeat them," Knox said.

"Them *who*?" I asked.

"The militia up north. Its' too big and strong. They'll just keep coming."

"Let me worry about that."

Chapter 19

Gia scowled at me. I was trying to remain unfazed in the face of her disdain, but it was a challenge. Time was ticking. "I'm sorry you're still pissed off I drugged you," I told her. "I had no choice. You were uncooperative. If you want me to treat you differently, be cooperative, like I'm asking."

We were all set to leave the dome.

Curtis and Tim had been given a dose of the blue stuff, something Walt had named Quell, and were secured. Both men were awake, but unmoving. They seemed sleepy and content, actual smiles on their faces. I hope it lasted. Walt had said he'd used it only a few times, but he had more than enough for another dose and was going to keep a constant watch, backed up by Daze and Knox—and Gia if she decided to cooperate.

That was still up for debate.

"I don't believe you," Gia said.

I leaned forward. We were sitting in a pair of

chairs across from each other. She had woken up ten minutes ago. "What's not to believe?" I said. "You and Knox, from what he's told us while you were out, sound like the perfect pair to be in charge of the new tribe once we're gone." The *new* tribe would consist of the remaining scientists and anyone Knox deemed trustworthy. We'd decided to incarcerate the rest until we returned with reinforcements from the city. It was the best plan we had.

Conveniently, this tribe had some sort of building they used regularly to jail people who pissed Jorgen off. He sounded like a lovely leader.

Gia sputtered, rolling her eyes. "And once you come back, you're going to shuttle us back to the city with you? Just like that? We won't owe you for any of it." In Gia's world, there was always a cost, and most of the time, it was steep. That was my world, too, except when I dealt with my crew. Right now, Gia, Walt, and Knox had become my responsibility, just like Daze—and anyone else who decided to go with us. But these guys didn't require the same kind of sustainer/sustainee relationship. They were adults.

"Your payment is keeping the scientists safe from both your militia and the militia that's trying to infiltrate from up north," I told her. "It's a huge job. In fact, it's so large that once you get to the city, I will arrange a place for you to stay and stock you with the necessary supplies." I was making it up as I went along, but the Emporium was big enough to house a big group until we figured out better accommodations.

"Why us?" she asked.

She wasn't making this easy on me. It was clear nobody had ever trusted her with much. "While you were asleep, Knox gave us a rundown of every member of your group. He said there are only a small handful who are against merging with the militia up north. You two, a woman named Bree, and two or three others—not counting the kids. Is he telling the truth?"

"Yeah."

"Do you think someone else in the group would do a better job than you two at keeping everyone safe? Maybe Bree, perhaps?" I had a hunch that giving Gia power would transform her, which was my goal. This girl was being given a chance to turn her harsh life into something worthwhile. I was going to do everything within my power to make it happen and make her see it *could* happen. I just needed to do it quickly.

"Shit, no," she said with an accompanying lip curl.

"Will you be able to protect the tribe against the militia up north?"

"Of course." Her tone was arrogant.

Perfect.

"Then there shouldn't be a problem," I told her. "You just confirmed that you're the right person for this job, and we need the position filled. You will be compensated for your trouble once we get to the city. Are we done here?" I made a move to stand.

She narrowed her gaze at me as I stood, moving the chair out of my way with a foot so I stood in front of her. "How do I know you won't double-cross us and leave us behind?"

"You have my word. That's all I can give at the moment," I answered. "If for some reason we don't return, you get to keep all this. You'll have Knox and Walt and the remaining scientists. If you pay attention, I'm sure the scientists will be willing to teach you what they know—at least enough to keep the tribe going once they're gone."

Walt nodded helpfully.

"We don't want to live in this shithole anymore," she replied unequivocally, standing, her body language aggressive. "I'll do what you ask, but the condition is you *have* to come back here and get us. No matter what."

"I will if I'm able, that's all I can promise. I have a crew in the city. As soon as we get back, they'll know your location and situation. If I don't return, they will. If nobody returns, it means we're all dead and you're better off down here—at least for a while. The city is unstable. Once we're there, we'll need to see to some things, try to make it a little safer. Then we'll fly down here and get you. That's all the assurance I can give."

Gia looked like she was going to argue, but Knox, who had come up behind her, nodded firmly. "We agree to your terms," he interjected. "We will make sure everything stays safe here until you return." He had told us about their bomb capabilities. The militia was well armed. It would definitely take the both of them, along with any others who were able to help, to keep the northern militia from taking over in our absence. But they had a good chance of success, and we had no other choice.

"Good," I said. "Then it's done. Case and I are heading to the first militia outpost, which Knox said is next to Tandor's, or Teddy's, home. We'll go to the next one after we check the residence for sodium alginate." Knox had told us that the militia members lived together and that most of the original tribespeople had their own area. Not every tribe member was going to cooperate, but we'd focus on rounding up the militia first. There were twelve, not including Tim and Curtis. "Once we get them secured in the jail building, we'll come back here."

Gia had her arms crossed, legs splayed. "I'm going with you. You may run into traps Knox doesn't know about. If you do, you're dead."

Knox had gone over all of the issues we could potentially run into. There was no reason for her to come. In fact, staying here to protect Walt was a better place for her to be.

But I couldn't mistake the intent. There was something more. I peered at her, trying to figure out the real meaning. "Are you out for revenge?" I asked.

She jutted her chin out. "So what if I am?"

I moved in front of her, getting up close. "I have no issue with that. Your past, and at whose hands you've suffered, is yours to deal with however you choose. I won't stand in the way. But if you join us, you follow *my* lead. Not the other way around." She gave me an infinitesimal nod. It was enough. I turned to Knox. "You stay here with Walt and Daze. Protect them with everything you've got." Walt had assured us he had plenty of hydro-bombs, so they could defend themselves if need be.

Case was already ascending the steps. I drew Gia's gun out of my waistband and handed it to her.

She took it with a grunt.

I tugged Maisie out of my pocket and set her in Daze's hand. "She should alert you if anyone's approaching, especially if it's not us. Isn't that right, Maisie?"

Her lights popped on, and she said, "Human signatures are all unique. Certain genetic markers include—"

"Stop," I ordered. "Not necessary to explain everything ad nauseum."

Daze's expression was solemn, despite my attempt to lighten the mood. "Come back alive."

"That's the plan, kid," I said. I turned to Knox. "Do you know how to fly a craft?"

Knox looked uncertain, but nodded.

"If something happens to us and we don't make it back, take Walt and the kid back up to the city. Daze will know where to go to contact my crew. They will help you." I turned and followed Case and Gia out of the dome. Once we were all outside, I said, "We're taking the craft these guys left behind so nobody will get suspicious if they see us in the sky."

Gia took the lead.

We jogged after her as she entered the path we'd seen before. A short distance away, the craft came into view. It was beat-up, possibly once a shade of gray, but so scuffed it was hard to tell for sure. It looked like a B model, the one that came right after Luce. It didn't have very many upgrades that I knew of, so she should be fairly familiar to fly.

As we got closer, Case said, "Looks like a B9, or thereabouts. They weren't known for much, just next on the assembly line."

"Exactly," I said. "That's why I'm flying." I headed to the pilot's side. Gia and Case headed to the passenger's. The inside was in slightly better condition than the outside, but not by much. The seats had stuffing sticking out, everything was filthy, and if Daze thought my stuff stank, it was putrid in here. I took a big breath as I shut the door. It wheezed out as I said, "It's too bad we can't fly with the doors open. Man, when you only have one craft in the whole tribe, it might be a good idea to keep it clean."

From the backseat, Gia said, "This is a rarely used craft. One we've only gotten working recently. All our other crafts were taken a few months ago by Teddy and his followers. Another reason why the tribe wants to join with the militia up north."

I punched the motor on, and it gurgled, finally sputtering to life. "Did you know Teddy well?"

"Not really," she answered. "He kept to himself, and he was older than me. He joined the tribe with his father as a small kid, before I was born. But he knew how to convince people of things, so people thought he was smart. I never did, though. I thought he was strange."

I took to the air. "That seems like an accurate picture of Teddy, although I only had one short interaction with him," I said. "Why didn't you go with him to the city?" There had probably been negotiations of who would leave and who would stay and protect the scientists.

A slight red tinted her cheekbones. She really was quite pretty, in an unusual way. Her features were broad and sweeping. She sat back in the seat, crossing her arms. "I couldn't. I was promised to our leader as a wife on my nineteenth birthday."

As we gained altitude, the motor sputtered and the craft undulated, but it slowly continued to rise. I wasn't going to take us too high. I didn't want to attract attention. "I take it that birthday is coming soon."

"It's tomorrow," she said.

Case had been quiet up until now. "Stick close to the ocean. According to Knox and Walt, the first residence is six or seven kilometers straight south."

I veered the craft east toward the ocean. I wasn't planning on getting too close, since the extra wind shear from the waves could bounce us all over the place. When we were stabilized over the sand, I increased speed. "Gia, do you know what this place looks like? I need landmarks. A place to stop ahead of the residence. My goal is to get in before anybody spots us."

"There are two buildings. Teddy's dome is an unusual color," she said. "It stands out. The other building, where the militia live, is a regular structure."

"What color is the dome?"

"Bright red."

"How did they achieve that?" I asked.

"How should I know?" she quipped. "It was always that way, ever since I was born."

"Are both your parents dead?" I asked.

"Yes."

"How old were you when they died?"

"I don't know. I was too young to remember."

Case sat forward. "I see something red up ahead."

I did, too. Any sort of change of color in this world and you noticed. "How far away should we land?" I started to decelerate.

"A kilometer at least," Case answered.

Because nothing worked in this crappy craft, there was no distance information available. I eyeballed it and brought the craft down on the sand, partially behind a dune. It was going to have to do. The distance was likely longer than a kilometer, but that was fine.

We all got out. It was a blessed relief to escape the stench. "Getting back into that craft is going to take some fortification, possibly more than I have," I said as we began to trudge down the beach. "How did your tribe learn to make these domes?" I asked Gia.

She shrugged. "They were designed by some engineer before I was born. We haven't been able to duplicate them exactly, although people have tried."

"Why didn't the militia take over the vacant one next to Walt?" Case asked.

"Because the old man threatened to stop making slurry," she answered. "He also told them he would set traps that would melt their skin off. So they left it alone."

I chuckled. He was a crafty old man, I'd give him that. He'd managed to stay alive and keep what was his.

We walked in silence for a while, though *silence* was a misnomer. The waves were crashing a hundred meters away, the sound thunderous, angry, and pounding, and our boots crunched over remnants of sticks and twigs.

As we edged closer, I noticed that the top of the dome was in disrepair. The red coloring was chipped, possibly eroded all the way through in some places. That didn't bode well for what was inside.

"Shit," I said under my breath. "That doesn't look good."

"No, it doesn't," Case agreed.

We all trudged up a short hill, finally coming into full view of the dome. The other structure wasn't visible yet. "Is the militia residence further inland?" I asked Gia.

"Yes. It's just up and over that slight rise." She gestured. "They will likely be inside. No one much likes the rain." That was an understatement.

"We draw our weapons now," I said, sliding out my Gem. "Case found tech phones on Curtis and Tim."

He'd brought one and left one behind. "It's only a matter of time before these guys start communicating with each other. We also don't know who else is out looking for you and Knox. It can't only be Curtis and Tim. When did you leave?"

"At dawn."

"When were you two supposed to check in?" Case asked.

"Two hours ago," she replied.

Gia and Case both drew their weapons.

"Since we're here, we investigate Teddy's place first," I said, making a quick change to the plan. "We have to see if there are any supplies left. We owe it to Mary. Since the militia are not actively guarding this area, we take our advantages where we can."

Case nodded in agreement, and we slipped down a short incline, navigating large piles of sand. As we moved closer, it was obvious the dome hadn't been kept up for a while. Cracks and chips marred its façade.

We eased around the side to find that the dome was missing its front door.

But that wasn't the only alarming thing.

Black scorch marks licked up the sides of the opening. Not only had it been damaged, but it'd been set on fire.

I lowered my weapon. "Well," I sighed. "I guess it's clear why the militia aren't actively guarding it. There's nothing left to guard."

Chapter 20

I turned to to Gia. "Did Teddy do this himself before he left?"

She shrugged, looking as confused as we were. "I didn't know it'd been destroyed. They don't trust me with shit around here. Knox and me are low in status for a reason—because we don't listen." I was certain she'd paid a high price for that.

"I'm going in to take a look," Case said.

"Why bother?" We didn't have to go inside to know that everything was destroyed. The dome had holes open to the elements all over and was lacking a door. So, on top of the fire damage, there was probably knee-high water from the constant rain.

"Because we're here," he said, holstering his Pulse. "My guess is Tandor did this. When he left, he took what he needed and didn't want anyone else to have access to his home."

It made sense, as Tandor had been an unstable asshole.

"Fine. If you see anything, holler." I kicked an errant stone big enough to hurt my toe as Case descended into the semidarkness.

According to Walt, there wasn't any seaweed growing anywhere and it was clear we weren't going to find any here at Tandor's residence. We had no way to access any sodium alginate.

"How are you going to get your stuff now?" Gia asked.

"We're not," I said. "There's no way to get it if it's not here. We knew it was a long shot when we took off on this journey. I just hoped we'd be successful. There's someone waiting for it back up in the city, and if we don't have it, we can't help her."

"There might be another way," she said quietly.

My eyebrows eased up. "What are you talking about?"

"Teddy lived with some of the scientists when he was younger. They took him in as a sustainee when his father left." She gestured toward the dome. "If he decided to burn this, he did it as a show of power. But he wouldn't be stupid enough to leave anything valuable inside when he did it."

"Where would he have put his stuff?" She had my complete attention now.

"With the scientists or Jorgen," she said. "My guess is with Jorgen. And if it's not with him, he'll know where it is."

Case emerged from the dome, looking grim. "Nothing left down there except water and charred remains."

"We may have some hope after all," I said. "Gia thinks Teddy would've left anything of value with the scientists who sustained him or with Jorgen."

Case nodded and glanced at Gia. "Where do the scientists live?"

"Not too far from the other militia outpost," she replied.

"And from what Knox told us, Jorgen lives in town, in the middle of things," I said. "So we check in with the other scientists first—"

A shout came from the distance.

We all eased around the back side of the dome, which faced the sea, away from the militia residence, our weapons out once again. Something suddenly dawned on me. We hadn't shared with Walt, Knox, or Gia any of what had happened in the city. I leaned toward Gia and whispered, "Has word gotten back here that Teddy and all of his followers are dead?"

By the surprise on her face, I could see the answer was no. "They're gone?"

"Yes," I whispered. "At least as far as we know. Teddy was the one Daze was referring to who got a hole blasted through him. There might be a few stragglers hanging out in Port Station, but we'll take care of them once we get back."

Gia was contemplative for a moment. "That will change things here. People who were fearful of Teddy and his followers will have no reason to fear any of them any longer."

The shouting was getting louder, the voices definitely headed this way. It was unlikely that they'd spotted the tribe craft, but it was possible.

Case nodded. "Time to move."

He crept forward, and we followed. Once around the dome, the three of us spread out. The area was hilly, and whoever was coming to investigate hadn't yet crested the final hill that led to the dome. I nodded at Gia to take the lead. She shifted to the right, slowly moving toward a small incline.

Once she was there, she lay on her stomach.

I took up the space next to her, unable to see past the rise. Male voices floated over the short expanse, closer this time.

"Curtis, come in, Curtis," a voice said.

"What's the matter, Sammy?" another man said. "They ain't answering?"

"No—"

A tentative voice crackled out of the phone, surprising me. "This is Knox."

I held my breath as Gia tensed beside me.

"What the fuck are you doing on the phone, Knox?" the angry voice that must be Sammy railed. "You were supposed to be back hours ago. It's because of you Curtis and Timmy went out that way."

Static. "I know, sorry." Knox's voice was barely audible to us in this position. "Gia got hurt and we were stranded. But Curtis and Tim helped us out.

We'll be back soon." Knox was buying us some time. The kid was smart.

"Hurt like what? And where the hell is Curtis or Tim?" Sammy asked. "You're not supposed to be on their phones. We only got a few of these things, and nobody trusts you." If they had, we likely wouldn't be in this position, as Knox and Gia would owe them loyalty.

"Ask them when they're picking up the slurry," another voice said.

"Shut up, Keegan," Sammy retorted.

Static.

I was certain Knox was trying to decide what to tell these guys.

"Everybody's here with me." Walt's voice wavered over the line. The old man had decided to take charge. "The girl was hurt badly and so was Curtis when he tried to help her. But I've administered aid. Everybody is going to be just fine. They should stay out here with me for the night."

It would be funny to witness the confusion on these guys' faces as they tried to process what the hell was going on. I turned to Gia, keeping my voice extremely low. "That's only two voices, Sammy and Keegan. Do you think they're alone?"

She shook her head.

Almost instantly, another voice joined the fray, this one farther in the distance. "What the fuck is the craft doing here? I thought Curtis and Timmy took it." He sounded both excited and confused.

"Are you sure it's ours?" another voice called, likely Keegan.

"I've got fucking glasses on. I see what I see. It's our crappy craft. But if the boys are back, they should be here by now."

Case came up beside us. "We go now, while they're still confused."

I nodded, easing my body up. "We incapacitate these two and wait for the advantage."

The three of us crested the hill.

The two men were below, talking on the tech phone. It took them a moment to register what was going on as we descended. My taser was aimed at the chest of the man with the phone, and I was ready to take him down temporarily.

Before I could shoot, a sound erupted from my right, and the two men were flung backward as a continuous laser line ripped through both their bellies.

I came to a sliding stop, my mouth falling open as I turned to Gia, then looked back at the bloody men lying on the sand. "That…that wasn't the plan."

She lowered her weapon, not looking at all shaken. "It was mine."

Chapter 21

We had to move quickly as two shouts came from the distance. There would be no hiding this scene. There was blood everywhere. The only good thing was that laser fire wasn't loud, so it hadn't alerted the other men.

"You know," I whispered to Gia as we crouched behind a fairly large dead bush, "if our plan wasn't your plan, it would've been nice to let us know." I glanced over my shoulder at the grisly sight of the bodies. If I'd known Gia's gun was that powerful, I might not have given it back to her.

She ignored me, instead making her way back over to Sammy, one of the dead guys. She plucked the tech phone out of his hand and stuffed it in her pocket, rejoining me behind the bush to wait for the other men to show up. Case was three meters to our left. "If I'd told you I was going to kill them," she said, "would you've let me?"

"Maybe." I shrugged.

She turned, spitting over her shoulder. "I hope they both burn in the afterlife. If they don't, there's never going to be any justice. Their deaths were too quick." Her voice held the kind of anger that lingered and held on. Those men had harmed her, repeatedly.

"Sam? You over there?" a male voice called. "Come up and see this. It's our craft, but Curtis and Timmy are nowhere around."

"Yeah," another voice added. "It's weird."

In my mind, the only good reason they hadn't rung an alarm to alert the entire tribe about any potential danger was because they weren't used to having anyone drop in here. It wasn't expected, so they were rusty.

Being rusty was going to be their biggest mistake.

"Do you know who those two are?" I whispered to Gia. She nodded once. "Are they going to survive?"

She held up a single finger. "One will, if he doesn't try to fight back." She stared straight ahead.

The men were coming steadily closer.

"Sam?" one called. "Where are you?"

"Is it strange they're not answering?" the other one asked. "Keegan, are you at the dome?" he called.

Yes, it's strange. You should be on high alert.

Gia tensed beside me, ready to spring, but before she could move, I laid a hand on her shoulder. "Let me take the lead," I whispered. "You can have the shot, but let me make sure it's safe."

She shook her head. "No, I go. This is mine."

She was up and over the crest before I could stop her.

Case and I scrambled after her, but she'd already fired.

A shot of retaliation followed a roar of anger.

She'd missed her target, and we were out in the open.

"Get down!" I shouted as I ran toward her, pulling her to the ground as I fired a shot off with my Gem. But the men were out of range. We had nothing to hide behind, no cover whatsoever except for a few brittle, dead plants.

The men rushed toward us, their guns out. Another shot was fired. It exploded in the sand next to me, shards of scrap metal spiraling outward. He had a Blaster. We were within his reach. But I *refused* to get shot by one of those.

"Gia, is that you?" one man called, slowing. "Did they take you hostage? Why do they have our craft?"

I assumed he was the more compassionate of the two. He was at least concerned for the poor girl. His concern would hopefully slow them down. "Tell them we took you hostage," I ordered Gia. "Then we wait until they're within range." I turned on my stomach, lifting my Gem, my elbows anchored in the sand.

"Yes," Gia called. "Help me, Kelly! They took me hostage." She sounded convincing to me.

The other man barreling down on us—the one who wasn't Kelly—had some choice words. "What the fuck do you think you're doing?" he said. "Where are my friends?"

"Your friends are a little busy being dead right now," I called. "If you keep coming, you'll join them."

The man didn't even pretend to change course. Three more meters and he would be within firing range of my Gem. Kelly hung back, trying to assess the situation. Smart man.

Before I could take down the forward progressing guy, Case's bullet found its mark.

Right in the middle of the forehead.

He dropped instantly to his knees, blood already streaming from his eyes and nose. No matter how many times I saw it, there was no getting used to that.

The other guy came to a stop, his eyes tracking from his dead compatriot, to where Case stood, his Pulse extended, to where Gia was rising from the sand, dusting herself off.

"Drop your weapon, Kelly," Gia ordered as she brought her laser up and aimed it at his head.

The man looked confused, glancing around like he thought a trick of some kind was being played on him.

"I'd listen to her if I were you," I instructed, standing next to Gia. "Or you're going to suffer the same fate as that guy."

"They've come to help the tribe," Gia told the man, taking a slow step forward. Kelly looked like he was in his early twenties at most, just like Knox and Gia. "If you cooperate, you live. If not, you die. Just like Marvin and Jorgen like to say. It's your call, Kelly."

The names Jorgen and Marvin seemed to snap the kid to attention. "Jorgen…will…he will kill you for this. If I don't try to stop you…he will kill me." His arm had been at his side, but he slowly began to lift it. His hand was shaky. I couldn't tell what he held, but from this range it would definitely have an impact.

I cautioned, "You don't want to do that. If you draw on her, you're going to leave us no choice."

He glanced between us, panicked, his arm almost fully up now. "I…I have no choice." His finger began to depress the trigger. "My allegiance is to the militia. I…I have to serve my superior officers—"

My Gem seared a hole through his temporal lobe, right above his left eye.

It had been quick and painless.

I glanced at Gia, lowering my weapon. "I'm sorry." My voice held genuine remorse. "He was about to shoot you. His fear over disobeying Jorgen would've won out. I saw it in his eyes."

Gia nodded. "It's okay. I knew he would put up a fight. Kelly never had a thought of his own the entire time I knew him. It's too bad. He could've been a good kid if they hadn't found him at such a young age. He wasn't as bad as the others, but he would do their bidding, no problem. He deserved to die." She turned and began to walk away.

Case was in front. "Are there any more?"

I followed Gia, who answered, "The other man assigned to this area goes by the name of Arliss. He is not always here, as he likes to harass the younger girls."

"Well, the Blaster made a lot of racket, so if he was here—"

Gunfire exploded all around us, multiple bullets at once.

Damn.

I jumped back, grabbing Gia's arm and tugging her over a short incline out of the way. We tumbled over the top, rolling in the sand. Once we came to a stop, I sputtered, "What the hell was that?" I spit tiny grains of sand out of my mouth. "Was that one person or ten?" Nobody I knew could shoot that fast.

"It's a military-grade machine gun from over a century ago," Gia said, brushing sand off her front. "It's Arliss' favorite. He treats it like his baby."

More shots sounded, then ended abruptly.

I maneuvered up to my knees to try to see over the top of the crest, but we'd rolled down too far. Case had been three meters ahead of us when the gunfire had begun. I hadn't seen which direction he'd gone. Maybe he'd been hit.

My throat felt thick.

Gia stood beside me, and we both began to move forward, up and over the hill. I grasped her wrist before we reached the top. "Let me go first. Case could be down."

She nodded. "I'll back you up."

"Fine, just stay low." The outskirt was a pain in the ass, but I was getting used to having him around.

"Honestly, if Arliss was still alive," Gia said, following close behind, "he'd be firing. He's got a mean streak that makes him nastier than most. If your friend was down, he'd be pumping as many bullets into him as he could."

That was a comforting thought.

"How does he even get century-old bullets?" I muttered as we made it to the top of the hill, crouching to stay as low as we could as we ran down the other side. At the bottom, I glanced around.

No Case, no Arliss.

"I have no idea," she said. "Nobody tells me anything, remember?"

My Gem was up, my eyes and arms sweeping the area. We began to walk, traversing another hill, ending up near the bodies of the first two guys Gia had taken down, but still no Case or Arliss.

"Which way is their residence?" I stopped, turning in a full circle.

Gia gestured toward the right. "Up over there."

"Lead the way," I told her. "But stay close." She'd been holding her weapon up, like I was, but I could tell her arms were getting tired. She had a telltale shake going on. Her muscle tone likely wasn't up to keeping a gun steady for such a long time.

As I'd thought before, they must not see very much danger around here.

We made a wide berth around the men.

Then Gia made a sharp turn and headed toward what looked to be a path that led up and over another short incline. Once we were at the top, I spotted the residence immediately. It wasn't a dome, as Gia had stated. It was a low concrete structure.

We moved closer, my hand on her upper arm to keep her close. She didn't shake me off. There was no movement around the building. We ducked behind it. I stopped, listening.

After a moment, I stuck my head out, calling, "Case, are you out there?"

A short grunt, followed by, "Here," sounded near the front of building.

"Is Arliss down?"

"He's down."

"Are you hit?"

"No."

I dropped my arms, letting out a small breath as I moved around the corner of the building. I was about to inform Case that coming to find us would be a good idea next time.

Instead, I stopped in my tracks. "What the hell is that?"

Chapter 22

Gia pulled up short just behind me. I reiterated the question, this time directing it at her. "What *is* that thing?"

It sat in a chair outside the entrance of the residence, positioned in a way that made it look sinister, its back sharply curved, head set awkwardly to the side—like it'd heard a scary noise and turned too quickly to investigate.

I knew it wasn't human, but my brain was arguing with me.

So many aspects were lifelike, including its size, coloring, and humanlike hair.

Except, of course, that half its face was peeled off, one hand was missing, and rubbery skin hung in ribbons in several places, aged yellow with time and stained red from the rain.

"That's Trina," Gia said, like seeing the gruesome robot was a normal, everyday sight. "Don't touch her, she's rigged. One of the scientists brought a LiveBot with him a long time ago. These guys stole it after he died and thought it would be funny to install her as their 'bot guard.' I wouldn't be surprised if they took turns defiling her."

"Don't worry, I'm not going near her," I said. I turned to Case, who stood right outside the doorway. "Where's Arliss?"

Case gestured idly into the residence. "He got spooked and ran, so I followed."

"What do you mean spooked?" Gia asked. "Someone like Arliss doesn't get spooked. He's the one doing the spooking." She headed for the door.

Case brought an arm up, blocking her way. "Don't say I didn't warn you."

She gave him a curious look and pushed his hand away. He let her go.

I raised my eyebrows, trying hard not to look at the spectacle that was Trina. "What happened to Arliss?"

"He put up a fight."

"As in?"

"He got more than one bullet."

Gia raced out of the house with a hand covering her mouth, her eyes rolling back in her head. She disappeared around the back of the residence, the sounds of her retching carrying.

Case's pulse gun was disgusting with a single bullet. I didn't need to see a body with more than one. I'm certain that what was left of Arliss would make Trina look like a beauty queen.

I glanced around. "As far as we heard, they didn't communicate with the other militia outpost. We need to get there before they suspect anything's going on. Let's head back to the craft." We began to walk, Gia following us. "You haven't told us yet why Arliss got spooked," I said to Case.

"He recognized me."

"You mean from before?"

He nodded curtly. He'd told me that when Dixon took out the militia Case had been involved with, some of the men had been out on runs. Arliss must've been one of them and had found his way down here all those years ago.

He might not be the only one.

Once we arrived back at the tribe's craft, I directed my next question at Gia. "If Jorgen doesn't live at one of the outposts, what does he do all day?"

"Not much," she replied. "He likes the attention of being in charge, especially after Teddy left."

"Does he have any predictable habits? Is he gone at certain times of the day? Does he do rounds?"

"Nope," Gia answered. "He likes to screw as much as possible and boss people around. That's about it. For the most part, he's a lazy SOB. But he's vindictive. Cross him and he'll carve you up."

"Tim said there were only five women in the tribe," I said. She gave me a curt nod as she settled in the backseat, then looked away. "Does he keep them prisoner?" I tried not to gag from the smell inside the craft. The stench seemed worse this time, if that was even possible.

"We each do a week," she stated grimly.

"Are you the youngest?"

"Yes, but not for much longer."

We'd see about that. I started the craft. "Why bother making you a wife if he gets what he wants already?" I asked as I lofted us off the ground.

She shrugged. "Because we practice the old ways here."

"Do the old ways include raping children?"

"Well, no," she grunted. "But as his wife, I'd gain status."

Status around here was a big deal. It was likely why anyone would agree to anything. Except Gia hadn't wanted it. She'd run a day before her birthday. I dropped it. No reason to keep talking about it, since it wasn't going to happen anyway. "Where do we go from here?" I asked her. "Where is the next outpost?"

"At the other end of town," Gia said. "Stick to the sea and you should be fine. Our artillery is located north, south, and west. Nobody has ever come from the east, so it's largely ignored. You got lucky with the way you came in. We have sensors and bombs."

"So we heard," I said. "What kind of structures are we looking for?" I veered the craft solidly over the sand, not gaining much altitude. We hadn't heard any communication over the tech phones, but that didn't mean we were in the clear or that these guys weren't expecting us.

"Two domes and another residence like the last one for the militia," she answered. "Two scientists occupy one dome. Another scientist lived next door, but he died recently. He'd only been here for about ten years or so. He had some kind of disease nobody could cure. I never met any of them before. I just know where they live, because I sometimes go on patrols with the men who live there."

I turned to Case, who'd up to this point been sitting quietly in the passenger seat. "How do you want to work this?"

"We go in the same way. Land a distance away from the structures and walk in. We take them unaware," he said. "If not, it'll be messy."

I nodded. "Gia, do you think the rest of the militia with access to tech phones believed it if they heard Knox and Walt's explanation of what happened to you and Curtis?" We had to assume others had been listening in. Thus far, there'd been no more dialogue across the line.

"I'm not sure," she answered with a shrug. "They should. Something like that's never happened before, but I don't see why not."

We had two tech phones on us, the one Case had taken and the one Gia had grabbed off Sammy. "Do you have more than one bandwidth here?" I asked her. "Maybe we're on the wrong channel."

Case drew the phone from his pocket as Gia said, "I'm not sure." She hesitated as she took out the one she had. "I've never had one before. They only have like six or seven."

Case adjusted the dial on his. On the second click, we heard voices.

"There's no way we can get out to check on them," a male voice complained. "They took the craft. It would take us hours to get up there, and once we did, it would be full night."

"I don't give a shit," an authoritative voice said. "Nobody's answering the phones up north. Something's going on."

I turned to Gia. "Is that Jorgen?"

"Yeah," she replied. "He must have his own channel or something."

"The old man said Curtis was hurt," the guy continued.

"I don't give a fuck about Curtis," Jorgen railed. "Arliss, Kelly, Sam, Keegan—none of them are answering their phones. I don't trust that scientist. He's been wanting to do us in for years."

"He thinks it's Walt acting on his own," I said, somewhat relieved. "He doesn't know we're here. That gives us an advantage."

"They're probably fucking Trina or something," the guy guffawed.

"If you don't get your ass out there to investigate"—Jorgen's voice was furious—"Trina is the only one you'll be fucking." How dare his subordinate not take him seriously?

"Fine, we'll start a patrol up there," the guy said. "But we're going to be walking, so don't expect to hear from us for a few hours."

"Do we want them out in the open?" I asked Case, whispering even though I didn't need to, as we were just listening in. "Or do we want to preempt, so they stay put?"

"If we can take them unaware, that would be the more successful scenario," Case answered. "If they're primed and ready to fight, we lose our advantage. There are three of us and six of them."

I addressed Gia. "What if you let them know that you're feeling better—that Walt fixed you up—and you and Timmy are on your way back and everything is fine? Do you think they'd buy that?" I slowed the craft, deciding to land behind a large dune. It was better to stabilize while we made a new plan. The outpost couldn't be too far away, since we'd already flown several kilometers.

Once I turned the craft off, I popped open my door to get some air. I was going to name this craft Stinky.

"Yeah, probably," Gia replied. "They might be a little suspicious, since I'm never on the phone, but nothing ever really happens here. There's no reason for them to be alarmed."

"What about when the militia up north comes?" Case asked.

"Oh, they always announce themselves. And Jorgen likes them. They bring him stuff."

I nodded toward the phone in her hand. "Go ahead and do it. Make sure the interaction is brief. If they want to hear from Tim, Case can yell something garbled in the background." I glanced at Case, who nodded.

"It's worth a try," he added.

Gia brought the tech phone up to her mouth and depressed the button. "Aaron, it's Gia," she said. "Tim and I are on our way back now. Knox stayed with Curtis. The old man is fixing his leg."

The response from Aaron was immediate. "What the hell's going on? Why were you out there in the first place? And why isn't anybody else answering?"

I twirled my index finger in a circle, indicating that she should keep it quick. "Knox and I decided to do a patrol out that way, but I fell down a dune and twisted my ankle." She shrugged. "When Curtis and Tim got there, they tried to help, but Curtis is a bigger klutz than me, and he broke his leg. We got to the old man, who is helping him out."

"Broke his *leg*?" Aaron snorted. No way was he buying this story.

"It was that dune that Marvin takes his skid board down. The steep one?" she said, nonplussed. "You almost broke your own leg there, dickhead." I gave her a thumbs-up. She was a natural.

"Why the fuck were you on my hill?" the one who must be Marvin interrupted, obviously listening.

"I don't know," Gia answered. "We were just messing around. What's it to you?"

"You will be dealt with appropriately." Jorgen's voice was cold and calculated. "Tim, bring her directly to my residence."

Gia took her thumb off the button. "Shit."

I gestured at Case. "Yell something when she turns

it back on." To Gia, I said, "Tell him okay, and then Case will give an excuse for stopping at the outpost first."

Case nodded once as Gia pressed the button. "Okay—"

"I need to stop and pick up a new pair of pants," Case called from the passenger seat, affecting Tim's tone fairly well, his hand partially covering his mouth. "The old man cut Curtis' up, and he's got nothing to wear. He can't go back to the outpost bare-assed. I'll drop her off when I'm done."

"Fine." Jorgen's tone was even more icy. "I'll expect you no later than half an hour." There was a pause filled with static, then, "It's too bad you decided to pull a stunt like this on the day before our wedding, Gia." His voice was eerily calm. "Your wedding dress won't be able to hide all the marks."

Gia clicked off the phone and tossed it on the seat next to her.

I grabbed her wrist before she had a chance to fully process. She fought me for a second, her eyes beginning to glaze over. "It's not happening," I said, making sure my words came out modulated and easy. My grip was firm, but not painful. I knew it was grounding her, keeping her present. "Gia, look at me. He's not going to hurt you anymore. This is our game and it worked. Without what you just did, we would've lost our advantage. You gave it back to us."

She met my gaze, her eyes slowly regaining their focus. After a few seconds, she nodded.

I dropped her wrist immediately, affecting a casual tone as I turned to face the front of the craft. "We owe you. That was a great performance. Once we get you back to the city, I'll make sure you get some coin. It's still traded up there."

She slumped back in her seat. "You don't owe me anything. And I'm killing that bastard. You can't stop me."

"I wasn't planning on it," I said as I eased out of the craft, then ducked my head back in. "Case flies, you're in the passenger's seat, and I'm in the back. That way, if anyone spots us, it'll look like you and Tim heading back to the outpost and all is well. Let's go."

Everyone else got out and changed positions.

The backseat was smaller than Luce's. Not that I'd ever spent much time in the back of my own craft. I struggled to get comfortable, not knowing where to put my knees, which jabbed painfully into the back of the front passenger seat. "Damn, it's tight back here."

Case grunted and started up the props. They shuddered and vibrated before gaining momentum. He lofted us off the ground, the craft wobbling. I prayed it wouldn't take us long to get there. I cupped both my hands around my nose and mouth, taking short, shallow breaths, trying to find some unstinky air to breathe. It didn't work.

"Go up there a ways," Gia ordered.

The craft eased to the right, the ride not smoothing out very much.

I refocused on breathing as Gia continued to give Case directions.

"Direct me to a place we can land out of sight of both the scientists and the militia," Case said.

"We already told them we're coming," Gia said. "Just park it where the craft usually goes."

"The minute we land," he told her, "the militia will know that I'm not Tim. If they all draw on us before we get a chance to position ourselves outside this craft, we lose."

"They won't be waiting," she said. "Aaron is too lazy, and the rest of them are just happy they didn't have to walk five hours to get to Walt's. Trust me, they won't be there."

Chapter 23

Gia was right. No one was waiting. We exited the craft immediately, not wasting any time. This topography was nearly identical to the area around Walt's home. The thunderous ocean was to our left. The domes and the militia residence weren't visible among all the shallow dunes.

"How close is the residence?" I asked.

Gia gestured. "It's down that way, around that bend."

There were too many bends around here. "We're going to have to go a different way," I told her. "The plan is not to walk up to the front door. We have to surround the building, and once we get there, you'll have to call them out." Hopefully, one at a time.

Gia had good instincts, but the kid obviously needed training. The thought of her and Bender working together made me chuckle. There was a chance Bender would meet his match. Nonetheless, it would be entertaining to see.

We followed her down a sandy hill and up another until the roof of the residence came into view. To the left, I could see the tops of two other domes. We were right in the middle of both places. I was just about to tell Gia there had to be a better way in when several shouts sounded nearby.

But they weren't coming from the residence on the right.

They were coming from the domes.

"What are you doing?" The older voice sounded a lot like Walt's.

"Just shut up and get on the ground," an angry male shouted.

"Please don't harm him," an older female pleaded.

"Shut up and do as I say," the angry voice ordered.

I grabbed Case's arm and Gia's wrist, tugging them both down so we were squatting. There wasn't any cover, so this had to do. "Do you know who that is?" I asked Gia in a hushed tone.

"It's Marvin," Gia whispered back. "He's in charge of this outpost, and he reports to Jorgen."

Now that she said it, I recognized his tone from the phone. He was the one who'd questioned why she'd been on *his* dune. From the sounds of it, he was hedging his bets that Gia had been telling the truth.

It seemed he might be smarter than the others.

"The only leverage Jorgen or any of you have over one another are the scientists," I said. "Marvin might suspect something's wrong. After all, you're being forced to marry Jorgen tomorrow against your will, which your intrepid leader reminded everyone on the phone. If you were going to retaliate, it could be now. But it doesn't matter. We have to help the scientists, whatever's happening."

"He had to have heard the craft come in," Case murmured. "You can hear those props from a kilometer away."

He was right. Stinky was loud.

"Will Marvin shoot you for no reason?" I asked Gia. "I mean, is he shitty enough to do it before he interrogates you?"

There was more struggling by the domes.

The old scientist called out in pain, and the female asked, "Why are you doing this to us?" Her voice quavered.

"I told you to keep quiet," Marvin ordered.

"No, he won't shoot first," Gia answered. "He likes to watch people squirm. He's pissed Teddy didn't put him in charge. He's Jorgen's second, and he abuses that power."

"Okay, it's time to split up," I whispered. "Case and I will enter from the sea, coming in from behind the domes. You go straight in. Act like you're confused about what's happening. But before you do, give us time to get there. Five minutes. We'll back you up."

Gia nodded as we began to retrace our steps, so we could get to the ocean unseen. "Stay away from anything that looks like a branch sticking out of the sand. They're bombs."

"Good to know," I muttered, turning back. "Don't

take out Marvin before we get there. Understood? If he's the only one there, we don't want to alert the others. We have to do this quietly."

"My laser is quiet."

"I'm not kidding," I warned, keeping my voice as low as I could. "Unless he draws on you first, you do nothing until we say so."

"I get it. I'm not stupid," she huffed.

Before she could give another huff of disapproval, Case and I were moving.

We headed toward the sound of the crashing waves, keeping the very tops of the domes in sight to the right. We could hear more shouts as we ran.

Case changed direction suddenly, waving his arm. "Watch the branch."

A lone tree branch stuck haphazardly out of the sand. It looked a little suspicious, but if Gia hadn't warned us, it might've been something we would have overlooked.

That wasn't a lovely thought.

Case and I slid down a steep incline facing the beach. The domes would be to our right about thirty to forty meters. There was more distant shouting, but I couldn't make out the words. "Once we get to the dome, you go left, I'll stay right," I said. "Once Gia confronts him, we take him down." Case drew his Pulse. I pulled out my Gem and HydroSol. I nodded to his hand. "Only using that?"

"I only need one."

We took off, avoiding another branch sticking out

of the sand. The domes were exactly like Walt's, with one closer to the sea and one more inland, but neither with bright-colored roofs like Teddy's. As we ran, I scanned the area but saw no movement. We rushed up the hill to the back of the first dome.

The voices were coming from farther away, in front of the other dome.

"You're going to regret this," an older, frail male voice said. "We're not going to take this abuse."

"Shut up, old man," Marvin snarled. "If you don't cooperate, you die."

"You wouldn't dare kill us," the older man challenged. "What would you do without all the luxuries we bring you? We keep you healthy and fed. We allow this place to be fortified with our technology."

"What's this about?" the female said.

I was waiting for the male to respond when Gia said, "Marvin, put down the gun. Why would you hurt these guys? What's wrong with you? When Jorgen finds out, you're going to be in all kinds of trouble."

"You don't look hurt to me," Marvin challenged.

Dammit. She was supposed to have a sprained ankle.

"What? You're the ruler of injuries? The scientist up north fixed me up." Gia's voice was eerily calm. "He put something on it, and the pain went away."

"If you healed that fast, why isn't Curtis with you?"

"His was a break. Mine was a sprain. That's why. We don't have a medi-pod in this town, so we make do. What are you doing with these two?"

We made it around the first dome and were starting around the second. It was clear Marvin was on edge. He didn't believe her.

"These two are my sacrificial lambs," Marvin said. Case was too far away to ask, but I was fairly certain that was an old biblical term. Something about killing the innocent.

"What are you talking about? Why would you kill them? And where is everybody?" Gia asked, her voice a few octaves too high. She was trying to make sure we heard. "Are you on your own?" The question had been poised casually, but I winced. It was too forthright.

The distinct sound of a gun being cocked came next. "No, he's not fucking alone," another, obviously younger, man said. They must've been waiting for her. "Do you think we're that stupid? Put your gun down before I kill you."

"Oh, hi, Decca," Gia said, still sounding casual. "Is Aggie with you?"

"Enough with the questions," Decca ordered. "And put your fucking gun down, like I told you."

"Where's Tim?" Marvin asked.

"He went to the residence to get pants for Curtis, like he told you on the phone," Gia said.

"Bullshit, I just come from there," Decca said. "I didn't see anyone. Something's not right. That's why we're here. You don't fool us. You got that scientist on your side, didn't you?"

There was no way to signal Case. When one of us

went for it, the other would have to follow. I was just about to make my move when a very familiar sound clicked right next to my ear.

The cold barrel eased into the crease of my neck, and hot breath landed on my cheek. "What are you doing here, bit—"

I pivoted, smashing my elbow into his face. He arced backward, surprised, as I scooped his legs out from under him with my foot. If Bender had taught me anything, it was to strike immediately. At the onset of a confrontation, there were only a few precious seconds before your opponent reacted. For some reason, most people liked to announce they were going to assault you, and if you were a girl like me, they always waited a few beats too long.

This guy could've benefited from a little Bender 101.

I mean, if he'd just shot me, I'd be dead and he wouldn't be lying on the ground looking up at the barrel of my Gem.

We'd made enough noise to attract attention, and I heard Case shout from the other side of the dome. I needed to get out there and back him and Gia up. I didn't have my taser out, and I didn't know if this was one of the men who deserved to live, so I lowered my Gem and shot him in the thigh. He screamed as I rounded the corner in less than six seconds.

Case had his gun leveled on the one I thought was Decca, since he had his weapon trained on Gia, so I aimed mine at Marvin, who had his pointed at the two scientists huddled on the ground. I could be wrong about who was who, but it didn't matter.

At first glance, the scientist didn't seem to be as old as Walt, but he was old enough to have been alive before the meteor strike.

"Where are your friends?" Case asked Decca.

"Wouldn't you like to—" Decca dropped to his knees, his hands going to his throat.

Case met my gaze, surprise on his face. He hadn't shot him.

"What's going on?" Marvin yelled, right as he fell to the ground, his hands scratching at his cheeks hard enough to draw blood.

Decca was rolling around, vomiting blood now. Gia took a few steps back, looking stunned.

I lowered my weapons as the female scientist stood, helping up the older man, who had more hair than Walt. She met my gaze. She had a weathered look in her eyes. "They're dying. It's okay, leave them be."

"There are still at least two unaccounted for, possibly three," I said, making my way toward them.

"No, there aren't," she replied. "Two are inside, and I believe this man took out one on the other side of the dome." She gestured toward Case, who nodded. "That's all of them. We warned them this day would come. They were well aware. This isn't a surprise. We were content to wait for it, knowing they would use us as leverage to wage their battles at some point, hoping to do this when we knew help was on the way. You're that help." She held out her hand. "I'm Nareen, and this is Elond. Walt told us you were coming. We welcome you."

I shook her hand. "Walt didn't mention he had contact with you." If he had, the plan would've most certainly been tweaked.

"We're scientists. We have our ways, and most of them are sneaky. He was only able to get us a message after you'd left his residence. If you're wondering why we waited this long, living with a militia—it's because it has served its purpose over the years protecting the area and leaving us alone, for the most part. But the game they are waging with the faction up north is too dangerous. Under such a brutal regime, our lives would be in imminent peril. It was time to act, and you came at the exact right time." She grabbed on to Elond's arm to steady him. He was at least ten years older than she was and several centimeters shorter. Nareen had a refined elegance to her, even though her nice, compact bun had been mussed by her interaction with Marvin.

Elond had a rotund belly, indicated that 3-D printing was likely alive and well in this dome. His hair was gray, not white. Nareen's hair still held a few black streaks. They both wore simple, homemade uniforms that were worn from age.

A moan came from the side of the dome where I'd shot the man in the leg. I called to Gia, having to say her name twice to get her attention. "I'm not sure who attacked me, but he has a laser wound to the thigh. I'll leave it up to you to decide what to do with him." Then

I addressed the older couple. "We need to get you inside. We still have Jorgen to deal with. When he can't get a hold of his men, he'll retaliate. If I had to guess, they contacted him with their suspicions before we confronted them."

"He will," she agreed as she guided the man into the dome. "But he's a coward. You shouldn't have much trouble with him."

As we followed them inside, Case and I shared a look of confusion.

This hadn't gone at all how either of us had imagined. But it was fine by me. These scientists might've just saved our lives. The militia could've gained the upper hand. Going into battle was always unpredictable.

I crossed over the threshold and sent a pleading message up to anyone who might listen. *Please let them have something to help Mary.*

Chapter 24

The setup in this dome was almost exactly like Walt's, except an area had been partially walled off for what I guessed was sleeping quarters, since I didn't see a pallet or a bed anywhere else.

That, and Walt's residence didn't have two dead bodies lying at the bottom of the stairs.

I stepped over the two men, who looked as though they'd been asphyxiated, based on their pale blue skin tone. Nareen was right, scientists were sneaky. I felt very little remorse for the dead men, knowing what life had been like for the scientists and the other tribespeople. It also gave me hope that the scientists would be able to fend for themselves, even just for a while, along with Knox, Gia, and any other member on board—if the militia up north descended while we were gone.

I glanced between them, Case coming to stand next to me. "We appreciate the help. I'm not sure if Walt told you, but the reason we came here was because Tandor—Teddy, as you knew him—arrived in the city with the intent to take it over. He was in possession of a quantum drive with formulas involving Plush and its possible cure, and ingredients, specifically sodium alginate. If administered early enough, it could help undo the effects caused by the drug." I glanced around the dome. "We had no idea we'd find you, or all this. Walt has made it clear that he'd like to join us in the city, when it's safe for us to return here and take you back. We're hoping that's what you choose, but we'll respect your decision either way."

Elond had taken a seat, and Nareen stood next to a table that had beakers scattered across it. "Yes," she answered. "We would very much like to come back to the city—if it's safe, of course. Heading into a big political uprising wouldn't be ideal. We barely survived one of those already." She picked up a vial and turned it over in her hands, which were long and shapely. They seemed like the kind of hands that were used to doing things precisely. "We've actually been trying to get back for years, almost as soon as we landed here. But circumstances have always thwarted us, and the years have passed quickly. We hope this time to make it." She gave me a small, bittersweet smile as she set the vial down.

If she wanted to relay more details, she would.

I nodded. "As long as we're here, I have to ask. You don't happen to have any sodium alginate, do you? We're trying to help the seekers in the city, but there's one woman in particular, an innocent victim in Teddy's games. She's only been infected a few weeks, so we're hoping her DNA hasn't been permanently altered yet. With the sodium alginate, our friend can make up a cure."

Nareen took a few small steps toward me. "Finding a cure for Plush was Candor's—Teddy's father—life's work before he deserted us for The Water Initiative. I never trusted him and always believed his motives were self-serving. I liked him even less after he left his son behind." Her voice was crisp and assertive. She would be an excellent co-leader with Gia while we were gone. "Unfortunately, the formulas you have in your possession, which came from Teddy, have been altered. They are not correct. Sodium alginate won't work. None of it will work."

For a moment, I felt like the breath had been knocked out of me.

The formulas were altered?

They were never going to work?

Darby had said that certain things didn't match up, but this wasn't what I'd expected.

Case picked up the thread. "That doesn't make sense. The sodium alginate worked on her when she was infected." He gestured at me. "Based on that alone, what you're saying is inaccurate."

Elond cleared his throat to speak for the first time. "Yes, if you administer such a cure immediately, as it's written in the formulas, you can avoid calamity." His voice was less shaky than Walt's and warmer than

Nareen's. "But it's not a long-term fix for those who have ingested the drug over a period of time, or have gone untreated. And each individual will respond differently to it, based on their intrinsic chemistry." He inclined his head at me. He had a bald spot right in the middle, but his gray hair was fairly thick along the sides. "You were very lucky. There was greater than a seventy percent chance that it would've done nothing for you."

The door above us opened, and Gia clattered down the stairs.

I needed to sit, so I headed to an empty chair. I had no words yet.

"The formulas had to be changed to avoid catastrophe," Nareen said.

"What Nareen means to say is that data was altered, on purpose, by us," Elond continued. "When Griffin Candor sailed away that day, he left us a gift, one that quickly turned into a nightmare. His son, Teddy. We tried our best with the boy, but there was something off with him right from the start. Nareen suspected that the elder might have been trying out some of his potential cures on his son, which meant he was also giving him small doses of Plush, which altered the boy's DNA years before." Jesus. Well, that explained a lot. "We withdrew a blood sample once, but found nothing conclusive, but we hardly had the tools to do a thorough workup of the genes. When Teddy became of age, he inherited his father's home, along with all the data he left behind. Teddy had a strangely brilliant mind, and he was able to piece together his father's notes and even revive some of his experiments. But it took an alarming turn once the militia arrived in town and Teddy discovered power." Elond gestured at the men on the floor to exemplify, I guess, the power shift in town. Hard to know. "We grew quite concerned, of course. Concerned enough to give the boy a sedative and alter those formulas ourselves. We knew he was planning something large, but just not what. It was our hope that with the formulas modified and ineffective, he would be deterred. But it didn't work."

"Since you altered the data," I said, hope still lingering, "does that mean you have the original formulas?"

Nareen pulled out a stool and sat, folding her hands in her lap. Her expression was stoic, her gray-streaked flyaways back to being organized in the bun. "We have the data, but it's useless."

"What do you mean useless?" I asked.

"As Elond already stated, the cures in Candor's research were flawed. They would only work if administered quickly, and even then, fewer than thirty percent would benefit. Griffin Candor fled to this part of the world many years ago, forced to exit the city by the government and his own guilt." She gave me a hollow stare before shifting her gaze to the ground. "He was the scientist who invented Plush, and its subsequent upgrade, which altered the fates of so many innocent souls. Plagued by guilt, he devoted himself to finding a cure for his disastrous pleasure drug, but he failed to do so."

Teddy's dad had caused this.

He was responsible for all the seekers and all the lives damaged by Plush. The information was a little mind-blowing, and completely unexpected.

Elond leaned forward. "The man became mad, plain and simple. It's why he left to join the Flotilla and why he left an innocent child behind." He made a clicking noise in the back of his throat. "Sodium alginate naturally attracts toxins in the bloodstream, binding them together efficiently. He was right to incorporate it in his work and was lucky that there was an intrepid soul here, right after the meteor hit, who gathered many samples of things that would've been lost otherwise. Word filtered up to the city in the years following the disaster that certain supplies could be found here. That's why we knew about this place. But for those poor souls whose DNA is already altered, it's too late."

Nareen rose. "I can see by the look on your face that this news is devastating, but all is not lost." She came forward and grabbed my hand. The gesture was a little more intimate than I liked, but I allowed it. "A scientist arrived here ten years ago. He occupied the dome next door. We lost him a very short time ago, and it's a terrible loss, because he was truly remarkable. For years, he refused to confide his story to us, fearful that if the government tracked him down, all those with knowledge would be killed. But slowly, over time, we were able to unwind his tale. He'd been working with a small team of individuals—brilliant scientists and people from the medical field—on a bio-restorative cure for Plush. This work began *before* the dark days."

I sat forward in my chair, my hand still in hers. "Why was he forced to come here?"

"Only on his deathbed was he willing to share the last of it," Elond said, picking up the story as Nareen dropped my hand and took a step back. "The government shut the project down. They decided to keep the Plush addicts as they were, deeming it easier than trying to cure them all. Too many mouths to feed, lack of infrastructure, lack of resources. But they were fearful that if the public—such as yourself—found out, they would retaliate. The scientists and medical staff were let go, but approximately six months later, they began dying." Elond shook his head sadly. "We have seen this narrative play out over and over again in our lifetime. Some factions in the government are just not willing to risk a thing. They would rather kill than leave a trail. And in this world, it's easy to do, as there are no repercussions from the law."

He was right. Whatever the government decided, no one questioned it, because no one had any power, and most of the time they had no idea it was even happening. "This scientist fled the city, leaving his family behind, fearing for their lives if the government came after him. When he fell ill, he realized too late what was going on. Everyone who'd been on the project had been given poison, mixed in with their protein cakes and ingested a little over time so as to not cause undue curiosity. Later, he verified that poison here and found an antidote, improving his health immensely, but the poison had already done its damage. Cancer ate away at him and ended his life ten years later."

"What was his name?" I asked, effectively blown away by the story.

"He went by Roman, but I doubt that was his real name," Elond answered. "He was a nice fellow, incredibly intelligent—smarter than most. It was a shame to lose him and his brilliance at such a young age."

"Did he say what government office he worked for?" I asked as my mind whirled. Claire had told us only days earlier that the majority of the government would rally behind a Plush cure, but there was one faction that might not, one that was so secretive she'd just uncovered its existence.

"The Bureau of Truth," Nareen said as Case and I shared a glance. "None of us here had ever heard of that department before, but then, most of us had been gone from the city for more than twenty or thirty years by that time."

"Did Roman give you specific details about the project?" Case asked. "Had they completed any of it? You said all hope wasn't lost. Does that mean we can still retrieve his data?"

"You're welcome to examine what he's left behind," Elond said. "But from what he told us on his last dying breath, they had been working on specialized medi-pods that would isolate and remove the damaged DNA, regenerate it to its original form, and reinsert it. Damn exciting work, if you ask me." Elond's voice grew animated. "Groundbreaking, especially at a time when the world was dark and science was at a standstill. Roman indicated that there was a sponsor at the start who funded the efforts and gathered the intelligence, and when he died, things changed very drastically. That's all we know."

Medi-pods.

They were working on medi-pods to fix the DNA that was altered by Plush.

I stood abruptly, my chair clattering backward. "Were the medi-pods ever operational? Do they still exist?"

Elond raised his palms toward the sky as I took a few awkward steps forward, my brain now pinging in several different directions. I stopped and fixed a less intense look on my face. It was clear I was startling the old man. "We have no way of knowing for certain," he stammered. "Roman didn't even know for sure. Their tenure on the project ended so abruptly he was only able to see early results, which indicated that some of the pods had cured at least two individuals. He never understood why they stopped the program. It would be silly for the government to destroy them, but who knows? All that amazing technology going to waste. It breaks the heart. On his last breath, Roman told us that after he found out that all the doctors and scientists had been poisoned, he took it upon himself to gather and hide—"

A small explosion rocked the dome, sending glass and metal tubes clattering to the ground and pieces of the ceiling raining down around us.

I swore.

We'd been so absorbed in the unfolding of this incredible story, we'd given Jorgen time to get here. In reality, he'd likely already been on his way, especially if he'd been in contact with Marvin. It seemed little happened here without him knowing.

I drew my weapons, as did Case, but Gia had been sitting on the stairs, listening to Nareen and Elond tell their story, and she was almost to the door.

"Don't go out there!" I shouted as she disappeared over the threshold, walking straight into whatever Jorgen had planned. "Dammit!" I swore as I ran after Case, taking two stairs at a time.

That girl was too impulsive for her own good.

A series of shots were exchanged. Someone screamed as Gia shouted, "You will never hurt anyone again, you bastard!"

I reached the top and was about to launch myself outside, when Case turned and grabbed me by the waist, spinning me against his chest as he pivoted, reaching out and slamming the door shut. I struggled in his grasp. "What are you doing?" I raged, bucking myself backward, clawing at his arm with one hand. "We have to get out there and *help* her."

He didn't say anything and didn't let go.

No, no, no.

Fuck.

Everything went quiet, and I stopped struggling.

My knees gave way, collapsing under me, and yet Case still held on.

After no more than a minute and a half, I found my footing again, my head braced against Case's chest as cascades of sorrow washed through me. "You can let me go now," I told him quietly. "We have to go out and see if there's anything we can do."

Case released me. "I'll go first."

I didn't argue as he pushed by me, opening the door.

What Gia had done had been selfless, but completely reckless. This world was hard enough, but losing someone never hurt any less. We'd known her for only a blink in time, but in those short hours, she'd proven her worth and shown us her potential.

After Case exited, I bowed my head for ten more seconds. Then I took a deep breath and followed him.

Gia had barely made it out of the dome. Jorgen—or what was left of him—was a short distance away. Case was heading that way.

I knelt next to her, bringing a hand under her head to ease off her helmet. Her eyes blinked open as blood rushed down her chin. Her chest heaved intermittently, bleeding from multiple wounds inflicted by a wicked Blaster, pieces of shrapnel protruding here and there. There was no way to stop the blood—there were too many punctures. I settled my other hand over her abdomen, stanching the heaviest flow.

She grinned at me, her teeth dripping scarlet. "He's gone," she whispered, coughing. "He's finally gone."

I nodded as a single tear rolled down my cheek. "He is. Along with everyone else who fucked with you."

She tried to laugh, but only managed a gurgle. "They didn't all try to have sex with me"—she coughed—"but they wanted to. I hated those bastards."

"I want you to know something." I brought my face closer to hers. "I put you in charge because you deserved it." Another tear rolled down my cheek. "I want you to hear it from me before you go. You are a strong, capable woman—everything they aren't. You always were. They didn't break you, they only made you stronger. And I'm not lying when I say you would've been the best leader this tribe had ever had, even at age nineteen."

"Almost nineteen," she whispered, her breath hitching. "My birthday isn't until tomorrow." She closed her eyes. "Tell…Knox…" I leaned down, my ear almost touching her lips. "I love him. He was the only good thing around here. Make sure he fucking survives without me."

I nodded as I raised my head, tears falling freely. As the fire in her eyes began to dim, I held on to her. I was sorry to see it go. She was as tough as they came.

She began to struggle in earnest, her chest rising and falling quickly as she tried to catch her breath as her lungs filled with blood.

"I give you my word Knox will have a good life," I whispered. "I'll make sure of it."

She reached for my hand, and I held it as she took her last breath.

Chapter 25

"You're quiet," Case said, turning to peer at me in the darkness. We'd been in the craft for at least six hours. Case had insisted that we leave at first dark to avoid any potentially incoming militia.

Daze was asleep in the back, but I wasn't tired.

Numb was a better word.

I opened my eyes. "Are you saying you like the sound of my voice?" I asked, tilting my head toward him. "Because if that's true, give me a chance to get my recorder out before you say that again, so I can play it back for you later. Without proof, it didn't happen."

"I'm just not used to it," he groused. "You haven't even demanded to pilot the craft."

"I don't demand, I tell. It just sounds threatening to you when it comes from a woman." I stretched my arms out in front of me, bending my neck from side to side. "You're doing a fine job. I didn't see the point." I glanced out the window, but saw nothing. It was still dark. Case had decided to hug the coast on the way back. "Do you think we'll find any clues in Roman's notes to the whereabouts of the medi-pods?" It'd been hard to leave before we went over everything, but Case had insisted, and I'd agreed. We couldn't do much without help. Elond and Nareen had accompanied us to Roman's dome, but there hadn't been much to see. He'd known he was going to die and had tidied everything up. There had been a drawer full of etch boards, a few nano drives, and some old-fashioned notebooks.

We'd taken it all.

"I'd assume so," Case said. "Elond told me that Roman told him that right before Roman arrived in the tribe, he hid away some sensitive material. Hopefully, he alludes to where he stored that stuff in his notes. It'll probably be in code, but I think we're smart enough to figure out the clues. My guess is he'd want the right people to know."

I lifted one of the containers Walt had sent with us off the console and raised the lid. The sweet smell of what I knew now was chocolate wafted out. I plucked out a cupcake and tore it in half, handing half to Case. He took it, and we ate in silence. The pleasure I felt as the confection melted over my tongue warred with my vision of Knox's face when we'd told him about Gia. The pain in his eyes had been shattering.

But the kid had rallied.

His sadness had quickly morphed to anger, and he'd agreed that between him and Nareen, and a few others, they could handle the remaining members of the tribe and whatever else the northern militia could bring. Curtis and Timmy were still alive, but I didn't know for how long, and I didn't care. What to do with them was the tribe's decision to make, not ours.

"From what Nareen told me," I said, "not only were we completely lucky not to have been blown up when we entered the town's perimeter, but they have chemical bombs set up all over. The northern militia must know they have that arsenal. After all, they'd been in talks with Jorgen and Marvin."

"Yeah, but militias don't just give up," Case said. "This isn't over, especially when they discover what Jorgen kept secret." Apparently, Jorgen hadn't revealed the existence of the scientists or the extent of the resources they had. He'd been waiting to hear from his boss, Tandor, before exposing the goods. Once the northern militia found out what was at stake, it would be an all-out war. We were hoping that we could be back down here to gather up the remaining tribespeople before that happened, assuming they'd want to return to the city with us.

Time would tell. Time—and if Knox and Nareen were successful in controlling the remaining tribe members. When the militia came back to finish their negotiations, which they would soon, they each had a role to play. If someone didn't comply, it would give everything away, which could lead to disaster.

"I felt better about them being able to defend themselves after Walt explained all their badass tech,"

I said with a chuckle. The scientists had means and were willing to do just about anything to protect their work. They had rocket launchers and remote detonators, gear that disguised body temperature, and various deadly chemical agents, like the ones Nareen and Elond had used on the militia. Plus, they had a pretty sweet communication system between the domes, which were going to be the new bases.

I yawned, weariness creeping in. "Walt giving us Babble blew my mind." Four vials were tucked safely inside the console unit.

"Tandor had to have gotten it from someplace," Case replied.

"Yeah, but Walt knows how to *make* it. That's next-level stuff. If the government finds out, it's going to be insane. We have to keep it quiet at all costs." There was no way I was going to allow the government to use Babble on innocent people again. "The priority once we're back is to find those medi-pods Roman was working on, if they still exist. It's our only chance of helping Mary and all the other seekers. I still can't believe the formulas Tandor had on the quantum drive are all worthless. But if we'd known, we never would've come down here in search of the sodium alginate." And what we'd uncovered was going to change the future of every human for the better.

"It sounded like Teddy Candor never had a full grasp on reality," Case said.

Maisie's voice carried from the backseat. "I detect seven like signatures."

Daze didn't stir, which I was thankful for. The kid was beat and needed to sleep. He'd helped Knox and Walt with everything and had been so relieved to see us, he'd just about collapsed in my arms.

"We know," I muttered. It was the tenth time Maisie had announced that on the ride so far. We'd told her to stop, but she was choosing to ignore us. We could now add stubborn to her list of growing attributes. She was obviously trying to tell us something, but neither of us had the right words to gain the true meaning.

"We'll be in frequency range of the city in about half an hour," Case said.

"Good," I said. I was antsy to get a hold of my crew. It was going to take a while to convey everything that had happened in such a short amount of time. "I can't get the picture of Jorgen out of my mind. And poor Gia. I'm heartbroken her life ended so early. I keep going over things in my mind and thinking of ways it could've gone differently."

Jorgen had been almost unrecognizable after Gia's assault. She'd sliced her laser through him and the bomb he'd been holding. All that'd been left was a few scattered masses. I'd been happy *not* to make his acquaintance.

"I hear you," Case said. "But in doing what she did, she saved our lives. We would've exited the dome right as he lobbed that bomb."

"I know, but it's still awful." I wanted to make sure her sacrifice would be worth it. "We have to bring everyone back who wants to come, no exceptions."

"We will. Walt said that packing everything up would take about a month," Case said.

"It'll take us a while to make room at the Emporium." It only made sense to keep everyone together in a central place in the beginning. There were already bedrooms set up and more than enough workrooms. We weren't sure how many would choose to come with us, but we were planning on the possibility of ten adults and six kids. It was going to be a huge undertaking. The logistics would have to be figured out. "Before we can think about bringing them to the city, we're going to have to deal with the Bureau of Truth." The mysterious government group no one knew anything about. "Have you ever heard of it?" Case and I hadn't discussed it before. It was hard to wrap my brain around what it would take to infiltrate and possibly take down a secret government agency.

"No," Case said. "Dixon had contacts all over, and we'd been in and out of the city before, but he never mentioned it."

We flew in silence until Maisie said, "I detect multiple frequencies."

We must be within communication range of the city.

Daze woke up this time, yawning and rubbing his eyes. "Are we back yet?" he asked, his voice clogged with sleep.

"Yes," I said, drawing out my tech phone. "I'm just about to get a hold of Lockland and Bender. If everything went well with their runs, they should be back by now." I turned. "By the way, did you find anything in Roman's notes? You fell asleep before I had a chance to ask." Daze had been going over some of the written notes we'd brought with us.

"Not much." Daze scooted closer, leaning his head against Case's seat, yawning again. "There were a lot of references I didn't understand. But he was working on something really important. Those medi-pods would save a lot of lives."

"Did he talk specifically about them?" I asked hopefully.

"Only a few times," he answered. "But since you told me what he did, I figured out his reference to it pretty quickly. Whenever he wrote about it, he used the words 'domes dip.'"

"Domes dip?"

"Yeah, medi-pods."

"Sorry, kid, but I'm not following."

"The letters of 'medi-pods' mixed up spell 'domes dip.'"

I shook my head. "I'm not sure I would've picked up on that. Are you sure he wasn't referencing his dome? He lived in one."

"That was the best part." Daze lifted his head, grinning. "It was genius, because anyone who looked at his notes would think that, too."

"But you're sure he was talking about medi-pods," I clarified.

"Yes."

I didn't press him. There would be time to do that later. Instead, I brought the tech phone up to my mouth. "Jerry, it's Ella," I said. "Come in." I waited ten seconds. "Johnny, it's Ella. Are you out there?"

Nothing.

I set the phone in my lap. I'd try again in a minute. If no one answered, I'd try a different channel.

"She was real brave, wasn't she?" Daze said, sitting back in his seat. I knew who he was talking about. Gia was on all of our minds. Her death had been hard news all around.

"The bravest," I agreed. "She rushed out there and took Jorgen out. She sliced the bomb he was holding in half, setting it off before he could throw it. She saved our lives. She's a hero."

"I hope Knox isn't too sad," he said quietly.

"It will be hard for him, but I promised Gia we would help him, and we will," I said. "Coming up to the city will help take his mind off things. It'll be a whole new life for him."

"How are we going to get all their stuff back?" the kid asked. "Walt has a lot of breakable things."

"We're going to borrow the mover drone from Port Station," I said. Heavy emphasis on the word *borrow*—meaning steal if we had to, meaning co-opt as our own. We had to figure out what was happening in Port Station anyway. So we either took it then, or since we knew where it was located—outside the guard station—it wouldn't be too hard to commandeer when we needed to. Once we had it, Lockland would tell his contacts we'd return it when we were done. Whether we did so was up for debate. "We'll also have Case's, Bender's, and Lockland's crafts. With the mover drone, that should be enough, at least for the initial round."

A crackle came from my phone, followed by, "It's Jerry." Lockland's voice filled the craft. "Where are you?"

I plucked up the phone quickly. "On our way home." I made sure to keep my voice measured, and I knew both Bender and Lockland would take note. My cadence indicated we were all fine.

"Breakfast tomorrow," Bender growled. "Success was marginal."

"Got it," I said. That meant they'd come up short. "Ours was…interesting. How's Aaron's mom?" Aaron was Darby's handle on this particular channel. I was asking about Mary.

"Stable," Lockland replied.

I was relieved to hear she wasn't worse. They were giving us till morning, because they didn't have much to share. We were beat, not having had a full night's sleep in almost forty-eight hours. Sleeping propped up in a craft didn't count. Before I ended the communication, I said, "I have a lead on a residence for my extended family." We didn't have enough code for me to explain everything, but this was enough to let them know that something was up and information would be forthcoming.

"I look forward to hearing about it?" Lockland's voice rose at the end to make it a question, which meant he was curious. "Let's follow up in the morning. I'm on my way out to get a haircut."

That got my attention. I sat up. Lockland cut his own hair.

Lockland was telling me he was being followed.

If he needed help, he would've asked. "Same time, same place?" I asked.

"Yep." Then he signed off, the phone going dark.

"What did the haircut mean?" Case asked, not fooled.

"Someone's following him." No use trying to keep information from Case. He was in it now.

"Do you think it's some of Tandor's men?" Daze asked, anxiety front and center.

I turned to make eye contact, just so we were clear. "If Lockland thought it was an emergency, he would've elaborated. Did you hear the tone of his voice? Tone, speed—all that stuff matters when you're talking in code. He was very careful to modulate his voice so I'd know it wasn't an emergency. If he's being followed, it's not aggressive." Yet. Being followed wasn't good news, though. "We won't know more until we talk to him in the morning." I turned to Case. "Head to the barracks. We're all exhausted. After a good night's sleep, we'll all think more clearly."

Maisie's voice filled the craft. "I detect seven like signatures."

I sighed. "Daze, can you try to find out what she's talking about? That's the eleventh time she's repeated herself." I opened up the dash compartment and took out the eye diffractors, handing one to Daze and setting the rest in my lap. "See if you can get her to say anything else about it."

Daze murmured something to Maisie that I couldn't make out.

Maisie replied, "AI intelligence needed to run compatible program."

I shifted in my seat so I could see Daze and the kaleidoscope of lights in his open palm. "What do you think that means?"

He shrugged. "I don't know. But when I put the Eye Diff next to her, she lights up. She's picking up on the software inside." He shook the diffractor next to his ear.

"It must be important, since she keeps talking about it," I said. "I wish we knew what to ask her. Hopefully, Darby will."

Daze brought the thing away from his ear and inspected it. He shrugged again. "He probably will. He's smart."

"Don't sell yourself short, kid." I smiled. "Your brain is very impressive. You figured out the domes dip, after all."

"Yeah," Daze said. "But that was easy."

Case angled the craft out over the ocean as I put the Eye Diffs back in the compartment. Case's sense of direction was uncanny. I was relieved to be back in a secure location and looked forward to a comfortable sleeping pod.

As Case flew in for a landing, Maisie said, "Hydration required for all three humans, Holly, Case, and Daze. Vitamin D levels critical. Seven like signatures need AI activation to run compatible program."

"Well, we can complete two out of the three," I said. "We'll have to leave the third until tomorrow."

Chapter 26

"Holy shit," Bender said, the remaining piece of cupcake sitting in his hand, his eyes locked on it. "Slurry made this?" He popped the last bit in his mouth and groaned, then ruined it by downing a couple gulps of aminos from the jug in his other hand.

"Jeez, way to flavor corrupt," I replied, chuckling. "Yes, it came from slurry. Apparently, the bio-printers we use need to have the slurry separated finely, like they did before the dark days. Walt knows the process. Now we just have to figure out how to do the same thing on a large enough scale." That should be easy. *Yeah, right.* I'd just finished filling my crew in on everything that had happened, ending with opening up a container from Walt and passing out the cupcakes, along with something Walt called bagels. They were soft and chewy on the inside and not nearly as good as the cupcakes, but they were still a thousand times better than protein cakes. "Okay, I've shared my story.

What happened to the two of you?"

Lockland nodded toward the Eye Diffs and vials of Babble I'd laid out on the table. "We keep this stuff at the Emporium. We're going to have to find a place to keep valuable items locked up tight. I'll get on it soon."

"Sounds good," I said. "I need to show Darby the Eye Diffs as soon as possible. I'm desperately hoping he knows what's inside them." Darby was still at the Emporium with Mary and Ned.

Lockland turned to Case, who stood off to the side with his shoulder pressed against a pillar. "Do you have anything to add?" Lockland asked. "The way we do things around here is go one at a time, so nothing gets missed. You heard Holly's recounting. Did she leave anything out?"

"Hey," I interrupted. "When have I ever left anything out?" I gestured at the outskirt. "I resent that. I've been giving detailed reports since I was ten years old. Nothing's changed." I crossed my arms.

"She didn't leave anything out," Case answered.

Lockland ran a hand over his face. He was tired. "I didn't mean it like that," he said gently, mollifying me somewhat. "You guys weren't together the whole time. I want everything you've got."

"Then phrase it like that next time," I said. "And while you're at it, ask the kid. He spent time alone with Knox and Walt."

Lockland addressed Daze, who sat on a stool near the table with Maisie. "Anything to add to the report?"

he asked. "Was Walt talkative while you were there?"

Daze straightened, giving Lockland his full attention. "He talked about some of his experiments. He perfected the slurry and was also working on some sort of laser technology. That's about it. Knox talked about the tribe and when the militia members came. He was worried about Gia. Nothing important."

Lockland nodded, satisfied. "How did the status egg work for you?"

Daze brightened. "She's great. We found out she can learn, and she has lots of memory and LiveBot technology. I named her Maisie. She keeps talking about 'like signatures,' but we don't know what she means. Walt knew about her software and made her make the sound of a horse. It was cool."

I cleared my throat. "Like I said before, the egg was helpful. She saved our skin a couple of times. It was a very generous gift. The scope of what she can do is vast and yet to be uncovered." I nodded toward Daze. "It's time to give her back to Lockland and thank him for letting us borrow her."

Daze gathered her up. "She can be touched without the cloth. She's durable. Walt showed us. Thank you. I hope I find one of my own someday. LiveBot technology is amazing."

"As long as it's not sitting out in the rain for twenty years," I said, conjuring the horrid image of Trina with the peeling skin and missing hair.

Lockland shook his head. "You keep it, kid. You can do more with it than I can. I don't have time to mess with it right now. If I have to go on a long journey, I'll borrow it from you."

Daze's eyes widened. "Are you…sure?"

I walked over and settled a hand on the kid's shoulder. "We don't question things around here," I informed him. "If Lockland wants to give you a gift, it's his right. Nobody is forcing him to do anything. Accept the prize, say thank you, and when you find something in the wild that's appropriate for Lockland, you can reciprocate. That's how this works."

"Thank you," the kid said sincerely, his voice cracking as he fought back emotion. "Holly's gonna teach me how to salvage. I'm sure I'll find something."

"I'm sure you will, too," Lockland said as he walked over to a bag he'd brought in with him and unzipped it. Without preamble, he tugged out a wad of black material and tossed it at me. "Bella was working on something for me, so I commissioned this. Turns out she had enough leftover material from last time and was able to finish it in two days."

I shook out the fabric.

It was a black synthetic vest with even more pockets than the one I'd had before. I smiled as I shrugged it on. "Bella's a genius." The fit was perfect. Bella had been making my clothes for years. I unclipped the bulky utility bag at my waist and began filling the pockets of the vest. It was extremely satisfying. "Thank you," I told him. "I was going to put in an order soon. You saved me time and energy, not to mention getting rid of this bag at my waist."

Lockland nodded as he began to pace, ready to begin his story. "My mission turned up nothing. There were no remnants of any sort of factory. Nothing but dead earth spanning kilometer after kilometer. I flew for three hours, turned around, and headed back. When I arrived in the city, I noticed a UAC hovering near my residence, so I set down and kept watch. It left after ten minutes." He stopped by the cooling unit, turning to lean against the counter. "I did some salvaging runs the next day, stopping in to talk to Darby and check on Mary. When I arrived home, there was an unfamiliar craft hovering nearby."

I had no idea where Lockland's residence was. It was safer that way. But I knew he had more than one.

"I decided not to engage," he went on, "and instead headed to another location."

We knew most of the crafts in the city. There weren't that many. "Describe the craft," I said.

"It was a Y4, black, new coat of polycolor recently."

That's all he needed to say. "A government craft." He nodded. As head of our security, if anyone had safeguards in place, it was him. The government had commandeered all the newer crafts years ago, so anything X, Y, or Z was theirs.

"If whoever was in the craft had tried to gain entry, they wouldn't have been successful," he said, his tone firm. "But, yes, it appears the government knows where I live."

"Have you talked to Claire?" I asked.

"Not yet," he said. "Reaching out to her could put

her in a tight place, since they're following me."

I glanced at Bender. "What about you?"

"I haven't been out since I got back," he answered. "But nobody fucks with me in my own neighborhood. Even the government knows that. But my location's not a secret."

No, it wasn't.

"I take it your mission turned up zero, too," I said.

He grunted before taking another slug of aminos. "There was nothing to find. Same story. Flew for hours, walked around the place Darby indicated, found no raw zinc, came back. Seems like the only other inhabitants in this region are down South."

I ran a hand through my hair, which was actually clean for once. I'd hit the cleaning stall at the barracks before we'd come here. "What we uncovered down there is bigger than anything any of us has been a part of before. And there's still a chance to help Mary and the seekers if we can find those medi-pods. We have some of Roman's research information, which I plan on giving Darby shortly, along with the Eye Diffs. We should have some clues in a day or two, if anything is written down. I have to believe that if this scientist was passionate about the possibility of saving lives, he would've left sufficient notes behind. Daze already uncovered one code—the domes dip—so, if there's one, there are likely more."

"I agree," Lockland said. "If what Elond told Case was true, that before Roman escaped the city, he took pains to hide information someplace secure, that says to me he would leave clues about where to find it." Lockland addressed Case. "Did Elond say any more?"

"Nothing specific." Case shifted his position next to the pillar. "Roman never told them where he hid the information, because he didn't want to put them in jeopardy if the government ever found their tribe. But I believe, like Holly, that he put clues in his notes. That's the only lead we have at the moment."

"Who was this Roman anyway?" Bender asked. "He was younger than the other scientists, right?"

"They don't think Roman was his real name," I said. "But, yes, he'd only been there for about ten years, which would have made him easily twenty years younger than the others."

Maisie's voice cut in. "LiveBot-compatible technology has specific signatures and needs to be accessed as AI. Mapping capabilities detected."

That was new. "What mapping, Maisie?" I asked as I moved toward her and Daze.

"Map," she replied. "A diagram of an area of land, depicting physical features, such as roads—"

"Yes, I know what a map is, thank you," I cut her off, turning to the group. "She's learning from us, hearing our conversations, but clearly hasn't found her stride yet. Either that, or we just don't know what commands to give her to make her work optimally."

"It's best to get her to Darby. He should be able to help," Lockland said. "The only thing we have left to discuss here is the threat of the growing militia down South and updates about Port Station."

"Did anything happen with Port Station while we were gone?" I asked, taking a seat on a stool. "Claire mentioned she was going to send some government people in to investigate."

"She did," Bender said. "And they didn't turn up anything unusual."

"What does that mean?" I asked. "If the guards are being threatened, they're not going to admit they've been infiltrated. They'd lie."

"I was able to get a hold of two of my former contacts," Lockland said. *Contacts* was another word for people he'd bribed. "They got back to me yesterday. One of them offered nothing, or had no clue if anything was amiss, which could be the truth if they've kept the overall situation on a need-to-know basis. The other said that once we took out Hutch and his group, the handful of guys who came to town with Tandor fled and Port Station has been cleared and is returning to normal."

"Fled where?" I asked.

Lockland shrugged. "That's an unknown at the moment."

"Well, it's a relief we don't have to go in there and fight, but that's not the kind of unknown I like." Not knowing where the rest of Tandor's men were, or how many there were, was troublesome. "We're going to have to *borrow* Port Station's mover drone to get Walt and the other scientists and their stuff back up here. Tactically, we can make a grab at blackout and take it with minimal issues, or you can just bribe someone with the promise we'll return it when we're done."

"I'll decide on that later," Lockland said. "It's going to take a lot of prep to get the scientists and all the people back up here without anyone knowing, which is mandatory. We keep this between us. I'll start on a preliminary plan as soon as we break this meeting." His expression turned dark. "Unfortunately, the government will have to be factored in at every turn. We have to figure out who's following me and deal with it. Then we have to decide what to do about the Bureau of Truth."

I nodded. "The bureau is definitely the biggest obstacle in our way." And would be the hardest to eliminate. We had no idea what we were up against, and I was guessing the threat would be substantial. "I'm hoping Claire was able to gather information while we were gone. Hopefully, once we figure out what their agenda is, things will become clearer. I promised Walt and Knox that we would return no later than a month. The threat of the militia for them is real. They have enough weaponry to last for a while, but as Case indicated, the militia will never give up, and if they discover what Jorgen has kept from them— the value the scientists have to offer—it will be an all-out war."

Lockland and Bender both wore somber expressions, reflecting how I felt inside. The tasks seemed insurmountable—the biggest we'd ever tried to conquer. But we would keep moving forward with the quest to succeed. And, if we did, the rest of civilization had a chance of success as well.

Change would be slow, but it would be substantial.

I spotted the kaleidoscope of lights before Maisie spoke. "I detect seven like signatures. AI-compatible, mapping advisable."

It was time to figure this out.

I stood. "We're heading to the Emporium."

Chapter 27

"Darby, you're killing me here," I said. Daze, Case, and I stood by his worktable in front of the pico. "I know it's a hard blow to find out that the formulas won't work, but we have a few more things to show you. All is not lost. Yet anyway." I mumbled the last part too low for him to hear. He had actual tears in his eyes. I'd never seen him so distraught. I drew the Eye Diffs out of my new pockets, setting them on the table in front of me, followed by the Babble and a small blue dart with a sample of Quell in it. "You don't have to cry. Roman has notes. Daze already figured out some of the codes."

"I'm not crying," he insisted, swiping at his eyes with his shirt sleeve. "I just can't believe all this work was for nothing." He gestured to the pico, which displayed the formulas on the screen. "The amount of time and effort that went into figuring all this out had to have taken him years. And they did work on a certain level. You just had to get the cure into the person before Plush could alter DNA. It makes sense, if you think about it."

Before I could reply, Maisie's muffled voice came from inside Daze's pocket. "I detect seven like signatures."

Darby's eyes widened as they shot toward Daze's bottom half. "What was that?" Darby stood, his legs a little quaky.

"Easy there, Darb," I cautioned, grabbing his arm to steady him. "We were saving the best for last." I motioned for Daze to come forward. "Lockland gave us a particular gift before we left." I nodded at Daze to pull her out. "It's a working status reader."

To say Darby was shocked was an understatement. He paled further as his mouth fell open. "I've…I've been hoping my entire life to find one."

Daze handed it to him carefully. "This one has LiveBot software, and she's adaptable," Daze told him proudly. "She's been learning from us. I named her Maisie. Walt says she's got a lot of memory, but I haven't been able to access much of it yet. I bet you know how to do that better than me."

"Don't sell yourself short," I said. "You were the one who set her free, remember?"

The egg lit up in Darby's palm, mesmerizing him even more, before she repeated, "I detect seven like signatures."

"She's been saying this for a long time," I said. "She usually does it when she's near the Eye Diffs, but not always. We think they have software inside, and when she says 'like signatures,' she's comparing them to herself or something. She's also said, 'Computer software detected in the form of artificial intelligence. LiveBot-compatible, not enhanced.'" I shrugged. "But we have no idea what she's talking about."

"This is truly incredible," Darby finally managed. "The things she'll be able to access and the questions that she can answer are staggering." He glanced at me, openmouthed, his gaze wandering somewhere over my right shoulder. "It's like having an auditorium full of history books at your fingertips. It's unfathomable."

When he continued to stare over my shoulder, I clapped my hands lightly in front of him. "Darby, I know this is big news. But now is not the time to become nonverbal. We have to figure out why she keeps saying this when she's around the Eye Diffs. If these have software inside"—I picked one up and shook it near my ear again, hearing faint movement for the first time—"why are they considered compatible with artificial intelligence or LiveBot technology?"

Darby came back to the land of the living, blinking a few times. "Right, right," he said, glancing down at the things I'd set in front of him. "The Eye Diffs definitely don't have software inside."

"They don't?" I asked, puzzled. "Then why is Maisie saying they do?"

Darby picked up a diffractor and twisted the outer covering, sliding it off easily. I wasn't going to mention that it'd taken the three of us much longer to figure out that same thing. "I've seen a few of these before, but they weren't in this good of shape. They were all the rage before the dark days. People were obsessed with changing their appearance. Bliss Corp had a line of high-end tech-centered beauty products." He spun the bottom, and a light flicked on. "But as far as I know, they don't require software to run them. It's a very simple process. The light laser does all the work. You just turn the dial to the desired color." He set it to green. "See? Then you put this up to your eye"—he mimicked the action—"which I'm not going do, because the laser integrity has most certainly eroded over time and would probably leave me blind."

I glanced at Daze who stood next to me and mouthed, *I saved your eyeballs.*

"Then you'd just hold it there until the light blinks out," Darby went on. "The cost to manufacture these was probably a few coins, and they sold for much more. People bought them up like crazy. Very lucrative. Where'd you find them?"

"In a remote cave. Someone had gone to the trouble of locking them up and protecting them." I opened the one in my hand and moved the dial. The light turned orange. Who would want orange eyes? Damn, people would do just about anything. I put it up to my ear again, because I had no idea what else to do. "But it has to have software—"

Maisie chimed in, "Software detected. Seven like signatures, LiveBot-compatible. Mapping capabilities specified."

"Okay, let's figure this out," Darby said, arranging Maisie next to the Eye Diffs on the table. "Maisie, please elaborate on 'like signatures,'" he commanded like a pro.

Maisie lit up, lights spinning. I wouldn't be surprised if she could sense a likeminded soul in Darby.

She replied, "Computer software detected in the form of artificial intelligence. LiveBot-compatible, not enhanced."

"See, she only says—"

Darby held up his hand. "Outline AI parameters."

She blinked a few times before answering, "Artificial intelligence specified for directional reference only."

"Define 'directional,'" he commanded.

"Actual locations within twenty kilometers of this static space."

"Who specified?"

"Program was designated by roman numeral one."

Darby asked, "Was the designator numerical or defined?"

I gasped as she spelled, "R-O-M-A-N space N-U-M-E-R-A-L space O-N-E."

Daze began to bounce next to me, reaching the same conclusion I had. Roman had something to do with this. It was too much of a coincidence.

Before Darby could say anything, Maisie continued, "Hard location accessed by AI chips embedded in hardware."

Darby glanced at me. "She's indicating that these things have AI tech inside." He picked up one of the

Eye Diffs and shook it. I heard the sound of something small shifting inside. "My guess is someone hid a drive in here. When she says it's compatible, I think she means that there's another AI chip embedded in whatever we're looking for. So when the two come within range, something will happen. But we won't know until we see the program, and in order to do that, we have to get the drive out."

"Do you think it can be read by the pico?" I asked as Case picked up one of the Eye Diffs and took the lid off, fiddling with the bottom. Daze did the same. We were all trying to figure out the mystery.

"There's a good possibility," Darby answered, tugging at the base of the one in his hand. "Again, we won't know until we see it."

When the one in Case's hand wouldn't budge, he withdrew his laser key.

"Hey, wait a minute," I cautioned. "We don't want to burn this thing up. If someone, possibly Roman, took the time to hide AI chips inside these things, they're too valuable to melt."

"This has been sealed professionally," Case said. "There's no seam. Roman went to great lengths to make sure nobody could tell that these had been altered. The only way I can see to open one is through the bottom."

"What about going through the top?" I said. "We could take out the lights, mirrors, and whatever else is there and try to access it that way."

Darby shook his head. "I think Case is right." Darby

inspected the top and the bottom. "If this is also meant to be a tracker, the AI chip is likely connected by a thin wire to the internal mechanisms, which is why you only hear a faint sound, instead of a more pronounced clinking, when you shake it. If you alter the lights and the mirrors, we could potentially break that connection. If it was me, I would've done the same thing as Roman, thinking that whoever found it would slice a piece cleanly off the bottom, making sure the chip could still be integrated once removed. We can't risk ruining the top."

"Okay." I nodded. "Let's do it. If we mess up, we have six more."

Case laid his carefully on the table so that a portion of the bottom extended over the edge, the laser key in his right hand.

Before he could make a cut, Darby said, "Wait."

Case stilled immediately.

Darby took the thing off the table and turned it on its end, lightly tapping it a few times. He looked a little sheepish as he handed it back to Case. "I want to make sure whatever's in there is at the farthest point away from where you're cutting. Go ahead. But only sear a millimeter off the end, no more."

Case took the Eye Diff back. "I'll do my best." He arranged it again, then depressed the key. Light shot out, and Case made a quick motion across the end.

A small disc of metal fell to the floor, tinkling as it bounced a couple of times and rolled away. Case brought the newly open diffractor up to his mouth and blew on the rim a couple of times, then upended the Eye Diff over his open palm.

A small drive attached to a thin wire dangled out.

"Don't touch it," Darby cautioned as he reached into a drawer for a small piece of cloth. "I should've thought of this before, but something that small is susceptible to corruption from any outside material."

Case moved his palm away, letting the thing hang in the air. It was less than a centimeter wide and so thin it looked like if you sneezed in its direction, it could disintegrate.

"Move it over here," Darby said. "Just a second, I have to get my macro-glasses. They're in the lab." He made a move to dash away.

"I have a pair," I said as I reached into my vest, withdrew my glasses, and handed them to Darby.

He donned them and bent to the task of separating the wire from the tiny drive, using the cloth to cover his fingers. The chip was so tiny I wasn't even sure the pico had a slot small enough for it.

After a few minutes of trying, Darby said, "Got it." With one hand, he immediately began punching a few keys on the pico. A small compartment separated from the top, rising slowly. He inserted the drive into a teensy slot and pushed it down.

Maisie lit up. "Passcode: Roman numeral one dash three dash seven dash nine point forty-five."

Darby punched in the numbers. No one was going to question anything at this point.

The pixels on the screen began to morph,

coalescing into a 3-D map of the city, pre-dark days. "Whoa," Daze said. "That's so cool."

We all gathered closer. "Look, here we are," Darby said, pointing at a blinking dot on the screen. "That's the Emporium." It was definitely the Emporium, because beneath the dot, gigantic letters that spelled out *Pleasure Emporium* were on top of the building.

The map had been interactive at one point. The user would've been able to map their coordinates, get directions, and access live pictures of the city.

Darby tapped a few more buttons, and a menu screen emerged.

"Can you tell what we're supposed to be looking for?" I asked. "Everything is so small."

Darby leaned closer, tapping in more commands, his nose almost touching the screen. "There," he said finally, leaning back and pointing so we could see. "That little dot. It's barely perceptible, but it's definitely the marker. Roman Numeral One used this 3-D map for reference on purpose, so we could tell the distance between things, which is pretty genius, since the world no longer looked like this when he created it. I think that's why he used AI, instead of just a regular mapping program. It can adapt, and it seems it just did, as it knew where we are, even though there is no satellite to mark our coordinates. It has to be responding spatially, which is incredible."

I pointed to the smaller dot. "That location looks like it's inside Government Square. Can you zoom in?"

Darby directed the cursor with his finger, and the

image got closer. He did it several more times, until the dot showed clearly on the screen.

We all leaned in.

"By the looks of it, that's inside a government building." Darby spread his fingers on the screen, moving them side to side, and the map rocked back and forth. "Look, if I lean it this way, you can see it's several stories underground."

I blinked, not believing what I was seeing. "Is that…is that a message on the wall? Enhance it more. Something's written there."

"I can see it! I can see it!" Daze said. It was like we were on a treasure hunt that was created by someone years ago.

"What does it say?" Case asked.

Darby was the only one wearing the glasses to allow him to see print that small. "'This location has been compromised and is heavily monitored,'" he read. "'Enter at your own risk. Medi-pod scheduled for destruction 05.07.2159. Uncertain whether they will enact.'" He sat back. "2159 was eleven years ago."

"Wow," I said as everything settled in my head. "We found a medi-pod, and if this is correct, there are six more locations hidden in each of the Eye Diffs. Even if this medi-pod was destroyed, like it says, there's a chance that one of them is still intact." I had to hold on to that thought. I took a few steps back and turned in a circle. "We have to get Bender and Lockland over here and open the rest of them. We only need one to work. If one works, we can cure people."

My brain began to go off in a few different directions.

"There's a chance they've all been destroyed, Hol," Darby said, his tone sober, bringing me back. "Each one of them could have a message like this." Darby read my expression, a low sigh escaping his mouth. "You're not going to take no for an answer, are you?"

I moved forward. "What do you think?"

"I think we're going to be visiting seven locations shortly," he said. "But how are we going to make them work if they've been destroyed beyond repair? We don't have those kinds of specialized parts, and there's no way to get them. I mean, I can only do so much."

Daze piped in. "Roman references the machines in his notes. Walt is smart, too. I'm sure he'll help you." The kid's voice held the hope we all needed.

"See?" I placed my hand on Daze's shoulder. "The answer is simple. We open those things up and uncover the locations. Then we go see for ourselves."

"And if none of them are operational?" Darby asked.

"Then we make them work."

DANGER'S CURE

A HOLLY DANGER NOVEL: BOOK FOUR

AMANDA CARLSON

Chapter 1

"Damn it!" I felt like kicking the side of the medi-pod in frustration, but that would achieve nothing. Instead, I turned in a circle, hands on my hips. This one was in worse condition than the last.

Not only had the government destroyed the project Roman, the scientist from down South, had been working on to potentially repair the DNA in seekers bodies from the effects of Plush, it had annihilated it.

The machines were in pieces.

"We only have two locations left to check." Darby announced what the group already knew. Lockland pried off the front cover and Darby began to inspect the internal mechanics. After a moment he said, his face directed inside the pod, "There's not a lot we can salvage here. But there are some pieces intact." His hands worked overtime, tugging out parts and dropping them into the box Bender held next to him.

"Do you think there's enough?" I asked.

"Enough what? To make a whole machine from scratch?" he asked, his voice muffled. "No. And the key parts—the ones responsible for the actual reconstructing of the DNA, in the form of precision lasers, have been completely destroyed. Whoever was doing the damage knew what to do."

Of course they did.

Lockland sat on a pile of debris nearby, his head bowed. We were all tired. We'd been at this for the last few days, working around the clock to find these machines. Not to mention trying to dodge strange UACs that kept popping up all over. "The last two locations are going to be the riskiest," Lockland said, which was also something we all knew.

"We have no choice but to go after them," I said, pacing the small room that used to be a lab of some kind. "We decided as a team to try the less fraught-with-danger locations first, but this is no surprise." I gestured to the broken medi-pod, which had several large dents pocked in the top, cracked glass, and a control board that had been smashed to smithereens. "They didn't even set any traps for us to find, because they were so confident in their destruction." This particular pod was located outside city limits in an old building the government had once used for some kind of experimentation facility.

Luckily, it'd been easy to find, since we had a 3-D map and an eye-diffractor-turned-tracker that blinked at us when we were within a thirty meter range.

The last four machines had been found in similar places, broken down buildings with no locks or traps. Sitting in a room just like this one, thoroughly destroyed and left to rot.

Case glanced inside the medi-pod. "The most likely place with a working machine is the one in basement of the government building—the same one we can't figure out who's controlling."

Our investigation in to the Bureau of Truth, the secret government agency who'd canceled this much needed medi-pod program, and had subsequently ruined these machines, had turned up nothing thus far.

It'd only been a few days, however, and I had confidence, especially with Claire on the inside, that we'd get a hold of some information soon.

Waiting wasn't my specialty.

In the notes that Roman had left behind after he died, at least five of the pods had worked while he'd been involved with the program. They had completely reversed the damaged DNA of seekers. Why the government had stopped the program and allegedly poisoned the scientists involved was beyond all of us.

Not knowing what was going on was infuriating.

Finding an intact medi-pod was the only chance that Mary, and all the other seekers had at survival. After flying thousands of miles trying to track down bunk information and nonexistent ingredients, this was the only cure.

"We know who's controlling that building," Bender said. "The Bureau of Truth. Whoever the fuck they are. They have to be the same ones who've been tagging us over the last few days as well." He was referring to the UACs that had popped up outside of his shop and Lockland's residence.

They were military grade drones, small, sleek, and hard to detect.

In my twenty-seven years in the city, I'd never spotted anything like them. It seemed they'd come out of nowhere, and it meant that whoever was manning them was worried that we were on their trail.

We were, but likely not for the reasons they thought…

DANGER'S CURE is available now! Don't miss out on the further adventures of Holly & her crew.

NOTHING IS CREATED WITHOUT A GREAT TEAM.

My thanks to:

Awesome Cover design: Damonza.com

Digital and print formatting: Author E.M.S

Copyedits/proofs: Joyce Lamb

Final proof: Marlene Engel

ABOUT THE AUTHOR

Amanda Carlson is a graduate of the University of Minnesota, with a BA in both Speech and Hearing Science & Child Development. She went on to get an A.A.S. in Sign Language Interpreting and worked as an interpreter until her first child was born. She's the author of the high octane Jessica McClain urban fantasy series published by Orbit, the Sin City Collectors paranormal romance series, the contemporary fantasy Phoebe Meadows series, and the futuristic/dystopian Holly Danger series. Look for these books in stores everywhere. She lives in Minneapolis with her husband and three kids.

Find her all over social media

Website: amandacarlson.com
Facebook: facebook.com/authoramandacarlson
Twitter: @amandaccarlson
Instagram: @author_amanda